"What do you think we should do about this chemistry between us?"

Cassie choked on her latte. "Excuse me?"

"I'm stumbling here," Braden acknowledged. "Because it's been a long time since I've been attracted to a woman."

She eyed him warily. "Are you saying that you're attracted to me?"

"Why else would I be here when there are at least a dozen coffee shops closer to my office?"

"I thought you came to the library to return the train your daughter took home."

"That was my excuse to come by and see you. When I found the train, I planned to leave it with my mother for her to return. And when I dropped Saige off this morning, I had it with me, but for some reason, I held on to it. As I headed toward my office, I figured I'd give it to her later. Except that I couldn't stop thinking about you."

Cassie wiped her fingers on her napkin, then folded it on top of her plate.

"This would be a good time for you to admit that you've been thinking about me, too."

Dear Reader,

CEO Braden Garrett doesn't have a lot of time to worry that his fifteen-month-old daughter is growing up without a mother—and even less inclination to start dating again. Besides, where would a single dad meet an interesting woman? Usually in the last place he expects! For Braden, that place is the Charisma Public Library, and the woman is sexy librarian Cassie MacKinnon.

Cassie loves her job, especially story time with the baby and toddler groups, and she adores Saige Garrett. Her feelings for the little girl's widowed father, on the other hand, aren't nearly as simple. Sure, Braden is handsome and charming and rich, but Cassie has no intention of getting involved with a man who's already given his heart away. Not again.

Although Braden and Cassie have both experienced love and loss, their mutual affection for his little girl might be reason enough to open their wary hearts again...

I love reading (and writing) stories about second chances, and I hope you enjoy Braden and Cassie's! And look for Tristyn's story, the next book in Those Engaging Garretts!, coming in May 2017!

Happy reading,

Brenda Harlen

Baby Talk &
Wedding Bells

Brenda Harlen

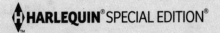

Recycling programs
for this product may
not exist in your area.

ISBN-13: 978-0-373-62328-0

Baby Talk & Wedding Bells

Copyright © 2017 by Brenda Harlen

HARLEQUIN®
www.Harlequin.com

Printed in U.S.A.

Brenda Harlen is a former attorney who once had the privilege of appearing before the Supreme Court of Canada. The practice of law taught her a lot about the world and reinforced her determination to become a writer—because in fiction, she could promise a happy ending! Now she is an award-winning, national bestselling author of more than thirty titles for Harlequin. You can keep up to date with Brenda on Facebook and Twitter or through her website, brendaharlen.com.

Books by Brenda Harlen

Harlequin Special Edition

Those Engaging Garretts!

Building the Perfect Daddy
Two Doctors & a Baby
The Bachelor Takes a Bride
A Forever Kind of Family
The Daddy Wish
A Wife for One Year
The Single Dad's Second Chance
A Very Special Delivery
His Long-Lost Family
From Neighbors...to Newlyweds?

Montana Mavericks:
What Happened at the Wedding?

Merry Christmas, Baby Maverick!

Montana Mavericks: 20 Years in the Saddle!

The Maverick's Thanksgiving Baby

Visit the Author Profile page
at Harlequin.com for more titles.

For Sheryl Davis—a fabulous friend, dedicated writer and librarian extraordinaire. Thanks for showing me "a day in the life," answering my endless questions and sharing my passion for hockey—which has absolutely nothing to do with this story but needed to be noted!

Chapter One

By all accounts, Braden Garrett had lived a charmed life. The eldest son of the family had taken on the role of CEO of Garrett Furniture before he was thirty. A year later, he met and fell in love with Dana Collins. They were married ten months after that and, on the day of their wedding, Braden was certain he had everything he'd ever wanted.

Two years later, it seemed perfectly natural that they would talk about having a baby. Having grown up with two brothers and numerous cousins in close proximity, Braden had always envisioned having a family of his own someday. His wife seemed just as eager as he was, but after three more years and countless failures, her enthusiasm had understandably waned.

And then, finally, their lives were blessed by the addition of Saige Lindsay Garrett.

Braden's life changed the day his tiny dark-haired, dark-eyed daughter was put in his arms. Eight weeks later, it changed again. Now, more than a year later, he was a single father trying to do what was best for his baby girl—most of the time not having a clue what that might be.

Except that right now—at eight ten on a Tuesday morning—he was pretty sure that what she needed was breakfast. Getting her to eat it was another matter entirely.

"Come on, sweetie. Daddy has to drop you off at Grandma's before I go to work for a meeting at ten o'clock."

His daughter's dark almond-shaped eyes lit up with anticipation in response to his words. "Ga-ma?"

"That's right, you're going to see Grandma today. But only if you eat your cereal and banana."

She carefully picked up one of the cereal O's, pinching it between her thumb and forefinger, then lifted her hand to her mouth.

Braden made himself another cup of coffee while Saige picked at her breakfast, one O at a time. Not that he was surprised. Just like every other female he'd ever known, she did everything on her own schedule.

"Try some of the banana," he suggested.

His little girl reached for a chunk of the fruit. "Na-na."

"That's right, sweetie. Ba-na-na. Yummy."

She shoved the fruit in her mouth.

"Good girl."

She smiled, showing off a row of tiny white teeth, and love—sweet and pure—flooded through him. Life as a single parent was so much more difficult than he'd anticipated, and yet, it only ever took one precious smile from Saige to make him forget all of the hard stuff. He absolutely lived for his little girl's smiles—certain proof that he wasn't a total screw-up in the dad department and tentative hope that maybe her childhood hadn't been completely ruined by the loss of her mother.

He sipped his coffee as Saige reached for another piece

of banana. This time, she held the fruit out to him, offering to share. He lowered his head to take the banana from her fingers. Fifteen months earlier, Braden would never have imagined allowing himself to be fed like a baby bird. But fifteen months earlier, he didn't have the miracle that was his daughter.

He hadn't known it was possible to love someone so instantly and completely, until that first moment when his baby girl was put into his arms.

I want a better life for her than I could give her on my own—a real home with two parents who will both love her as much as I do.

It didn't seem too much to ask, but they'd let Lindsay down. And he couldn't help but worry that Saige would one day realize they'd let her down, too.

For now, she was an incredibly happy child, seemingly unaffected by her motherless status. Still, it wasn't quite the family that Lindsay had envisioned for her baby girl when she'd signed the adoption papers—or that Braden wanted for Saige, either.

"I'm not going anywhere," he promised his daughter now. "Daddy will always be here for you, I promise."

"Da-da." Saige's smile didn't just curve her lips, it shone in her eyes and filled his whole heart.

"That's right—it's you and me kid."

"Ga-ma?"

"Yes, we've got Grandma and Grandpa in our corner, too. And lots of aunts, uncles and cousins."

"Na-na?"

He smiled. "Yeah, some of them are bananas, but we don't hold that against them."

She stretched out her arms, her hands splayed wide open. "Aw dun."

"Good girl." He moistened a washcloth under the tap to

wipe her hands and face, then removed the tray from her high chair and unbuckled the safety belt around her waist.

As soon as the clip was unfastened, she threw herself at him. He caught her against his chest as her little arms wrapped around his neck, but he felt the squeeze deep inside his heart.

"Ready to go to Grandma's now?"

When Saige nodded enthusiastically, he slung her diaper bag over his shoulder, then picked up his briefcase and headed toward the door. His hand was on the knob when the phone rang. He was already fifteen minutes late leaving for work, but he took three steps back to check the display, and immediately recognized his parents' home number. *Crap.*

He dropped his briefcase and picked up the receiver. "Hi, Mom. We're just on our way out the door."

"Then it's lucky I caught you," Ellen said. "I chipped a tooth on my granola and I'm on my way to the dentist."

"Ouch," he said sympathetically, even as he mentally began juggling his morning plans to accommodate taking Saige into the office with him.

"I'm so sorry to cancel at the last minute," she said.

"Don't be silly, Mom. Of course you have to have your tooth looked at, and Saige is always happy to hang out at my office."

"You can't take her to the office," his mother protested.

"Why not?"

"Because it's Tuesday," she pointed out.

"And every Tuesday, I meet with Nathan and Andrew," he reminded her.

"Tuesday at ten o'clock is Baby Talk at the library."

"Right—Baby Talk," he said, as if he'd remembered. As if he had any intention of blowing off a business meeting to take his fifteen-month-old daughter to the library instead.

"Saige loves Baby Talk," his mother told him.

"I'm sure she does," he acknowledged. "But songs and stories at the library aren't really my thing."

"Maybe not, but they're Saige's thing," Ellen retorted. "And you're her father, and it's not going to hurt you to take an hour out of your schedule so that she doesn't have to miss it this week."

"I have meetings all morning."

"Meetings with your cousins," she noted, "both fathers themselves who wouldn't hesitate to reschedule if their kids needed them."

Which he couldn't deny was true. "But…Baby Talk?"

"Yes," his mother said firmly, even as Saige began singing "wound an' wound"—her version of the chorus from the "Wheels on the Bus" song that she'd apparently learned in the library group. "Miss MacKinnon—the librarian— will steer you in the right direction."

He sighed. "Okay, I'll let Nate and Andrew know that I have to reschedule."

"Your daughter appreciates it," Ellen said.

He looked at the little girl still propped on his hip, and she looked back at him, her big brown eyes sparkling as she continued to sing softly.

She truly was the light of his life, and his mother knew there wasn't anything he wouldn't do for her.

"Well, Saige, I guess today is the day that Daddy discovers what Baby Talk is all about."

His daughter smiled and clapped her hands together.

The main branch of the Charisma Public Library was located downtown, across from the Bean There Café and only a short walk from the hospital and the courthouse. It was a three-story building of stone and glass with a large open foyer filled with natural light and tall, potted plants.

The information desk was a circular area in the center, designed to be accessible to patrons from all sides.

Cassandra MacKinnon sat at that desk, scanning the monthly calendar to confirm the schedule of upcoming events. The library wasn't just a warehouse of books waiting to be borrowed—it was a hub of social activity. She nodded to Luisa Todd and Ginny Stafford, who came in together with bulky knitting bags in hand. The two older women—friends since childhood—had started the Knit & Purl group and were always the first to arrive on Tuesday mornings.

Ginny stopped at the desk and took a gift bag out of her tote. "Will you be visiting with Irene this week?" she asked Cassie, referring to the former head librarian who now lived at Serenity Gardens, a seniors' residence in town.

"Tomorrow," Cassie confirmed.

"Would you mind taking this for me?" Ginny asked, passing the bag over the desk. "Irene always complains about having cold feet in that place, so I knitted her a couple pairs of socks. I had planned to see her on the weekend, but my son and daughter-in-law were in town with their three kids and I couldn't tear myself away from them."

"Of course, I wouldn't mind," Cassie told her. "And I know she'll love the socks."

Luisa snorted; Ginny smiled wryly. "Well, I'm sure she'll appreciate having warm feet, anyway."

Cassie tucked the bag under the counter and the two women continued on their way.

She spent a little bit of time checking in the materials that had been returned through the book drop overnight, then arranging them on the cart for Helen Darrow to put back on the shelves. Helen was a career part-time employee of the library who had been hired when Irene Houlahan was in charge. An older woman inherently distrustful of technology, Helen refused to touch the computers and spent most of her time finding books to fill online and call-in requests of patrons, putting them back when they were returned—and shushing anyone who dared to speak above a whisper in the book stacks.

"Hey, Miss Mac."

Cassie glanced up to see Tanya Fielding, a high school senior and regular at the Soc & Study group, at the desk. "Good morning, Tanya. Aren't you supposed to be in school this morning?"

The teen shook her head. "Our history teacher is giving us time to work on our independent research projects this week."

"What's your topic?"

"The role of German U-boats in the Second World War."

"Do you want to sign on to one of the computers?"

"No. Mr. Paretsky wants—" she made air quotes with her fingers "—real sources, actual paper books so that we can do proper page citations and aren't relying on made-up stuff that someone posted on the internet."

Cassie pushed her chair away from the desk. "Nonfiction is upstairs. Let's go see what we can find."

After the teen was settled at a table with a pile of books, Cassie checked that the Dickens Room was ready for the ESL group coming in at ten thirty and picked up a stack of abandoned magazines from a window ledge near the true crime section.

She put the magazines on Helen's cart and returned to her desk just as George Bowman came in. George and his wife, Margie, were familiar faces at the library. She knew all of the library's regular patrons—not just their names and faces, but also their reading habits and preferences. And, over the years, she'd gotten to know many of them on a personal level, too.

She was chatting with Mr. Bowman when the tall, dark and extremely handsome stranger stepped into view. Her heart gave a little bump against her ribs, as if to make sure she was paying attention, and warm tingles spread slowly through her veins. But he wasn't just a stranger, he was an outsider. The expensive suit jacket that stretched across his broad shoulders, the silk tie neatly knotted at his throat and the square, cleanly shaven jaw all screamed "corporate executive."

She would have been less surprised to see a rainbow-colored unicorn prancing across the floor than this man moving toward her. Moving rather slowly and with short strides considering his long legs, she thought—and then she saw the little girl toddling beside him.

The child she *did* recognize. Saige regularly attended Baby Talk at the library with her grandmother, which meant that the man holding the tiny hand had to be her dad: Braden Garrett, Charisma's very own crown prince.

A lot of years had passed since Braden was last inside the Charisma Public Library, and when he stepped through the front doors, he had a moment of doubt that he was even in the right place. In the past twenty years, the building had undergone major renovations so that the address was the only part of the library that remained unchanged.

He stepped farther into the room, noting that the card catalogue system had been replaced by computer terminals and the checkout desk wasn't just automated but self-serve—which meant that the kids borrowing books or other materials weren't subjected to the narrow-eyed stare of Miss Houlahan, the old librarian who marked the cards inside the back covers of the books, her gnarled fingers wielding the stamp like a weapon. He'd been terrified of the woman.

Of course, the librarian had been about a hundred years old when Braden was a kid—or so she'd seemed—so he didn't really expect to find her still working behind the desk. But the woman seated there now, her fingers moving over the keyboard as she conversed with an elderly gentleman, was at least twenty years younger than he'd expected, with chin-length auburn hair that shone with gold and copper highlights. Her face was heart-shaped with creamy skin and a delicately pointed chin. Her eyes were dark—green, he guessed, to go with the red hair—and her glossy lips curved in response to something the old man said to her.

Saige wiggled again, silently asking to be set down. Since she'd taken her first tentative steps four months earlier, she preferred to walk everywhere. Braden set her on her feet but held firmly to her hand and headed toward the information desk.

The woman he assumed was Miss MacKinnon stopped typing and picked up a pen to jot a note on a piece of paper that she then handed across the desk to the elderly patron.

The old man nodded his thanks. "By the way, Margie wanted me to tell you that our daughter, Karen, is expecting again."

"This will be her third, won't it?"

"Third *and* fourth," he replied.

Neatly arched brows lifted. "Twins?"

He nodded again. "Our seventh and eighth grandchildren."

"That's wonderful news—congratulations to all of you."

"You know, I keep waiting for the day when you have big news to share."

The librarian smiled indulgently. "Didn't I tell you just this morning that there's a new John Grisham on the shelves?"

Mr. Bowman shook his head. "Marriage plans, Cassie."

"You've been with Mrs. Bowman for almost fifty years—I don't see you giving her up to run away with me now."

The old man's ears flushed red. "Fifty-one," he said proudly. "And I didn't mean me. You need a handsome young man to put a ring on your finger and give you beautiful babies."

"Until that happens, you keep bringing me pictures of your gorgeous grandbabies," she suggested.

"I certainly will," he promised.

"In the meantime—" she picked up a flyer from the counter and offered it to Mr. Bowman "—I hope you're planning to come to our Annual Book & Bake Sale on the fifteenth."

"It's already marked on the calendar at home," he told her. "And Margie's promised to make a couple dozen muffins."

"I'll definitely look forward to those."

The old man finally moved toward the elevator and Braden stepped forward. "Miss MacKinnon?"

She turned toward him, and he saw that her eyes weren't green, after all, but a dark chocolate brown and fringed with even darker lashes.

"Good morning," she said. "How can I help you?"

"I'm here for...Baby Talk?"

Her mouth curved, drawing his attention to her full, glossy lips. "Are you sure?"

"Not entirely," he admitted, shifting his gaze to meet hers again. "Am I in the right place?"

"You are," she confirmed. "Baby Talk is in the Bronte Room on the upper level at ten."

He glanced at the clock on the wall, saw that it wasn't yet nine thirty. "I guess we're a little early."

"Downstairs in the children's section, there's a play area with puzzles and games, a puppet theater and a train table."

"Choo-choo," Saige urged.

Miss MacKinnon glanced down at his daughter and smiled. "Although if you go there now, you might have trouble tearing your daughter away. You like the trains, don't you, Saige?"

She nodded, her head bobbing up and down with enthusiasm.

Braden's brows lifted. He was surprised—and a little disconcerted—to discover that this woman knew something about his daughter that he didn't. "Obviously she spends more time here than I realized."

"Your mom brings her twice a week."

"Well, since you know my mother and Saige, I guess I should introduce myself—I'm Braden Garrett."

She accepted the hand he offered. He noted that hers was soft, but her grip firm. "Cassie MacKinnon."

"Are you really the librarian?" he heard himself ask.

"One of them," she said.

"When I think of librarians, I think of Miss Houlahan."

"So do I," she told him. "In fact, she's the reason I chose to become a librarian."

"We must be thinking of different Miss Houlahans," he decided.

"Perhaps," she allowed. "Now, if you'll excuse me, I need to check on something upstairs."

"Something upstairs" sounded rather vague to Braden, and he got the strange feeling that he was being brushed off. Or maybe he was reading too much into those two words. After all, this was a library and she was the librarian—no doubt there were any number of "somethings" she had to do, although he couldn't begin to imagine what they might be.

As she walked away, Braden found himself admiring

the curve of her butt and the sway of her hips and thinking that he might have spent a lot more time in the library
as a kid if there had been a librarian like Miss MacKinnon to help him navigate the book stacks.

Chapter Two

By the time he managed to drag Saige away from the trains and find the Bronte Room, there were several other parents and children already there—along with Cassie MacKinnon. Apparently one of the "somethings" that she did at the library was lead the stories, songs and games at Baby Talk.

She nodded to him as he entered the room and gestured to an empty place in the circle. "Have a seat," she invited.

Except there were no seats. All of the moms—and yes, they were *all* moms, there wasn't another XY chromosome anywhere to be found, unless it was tucked away in a diaper—were sitting on the beige Berber carpet. He lowered himself to the floor, certain he looked as awkward as he felt as he attempted to cross his legs.

"Did you bring your pillow, Mr. Garrett?"

"Pillow?" he echoed. His mother hadn't said anything about a pillow, but when he looked around, he saw that all of the moms had square pillows underneath their babies.

"I've got an extra that you can borrow," she said, opening a cabinet to retrieve a big pink square with an enormous daisy embroidered on it.

He managed not to grimace as he thanked her and set the pillow on the floor, then sat Saige down on top of it. She immediately began to clap her hands, excited to begin.

Ellen had told him that Baby Talk was for infants up to eighteen months of age, and looking around, he guessed that his daughter was one of the oldest in the room. A quick glance confirmed that the moms were of various ages, as well. The one thing they had in common: they were all checking out the lone male in the room.

He focused on Cassie, eager to get the class started and finished.

What he learned during the thirty-minute session was that the librarian had a lot more patience than he did. Even when there were babies crying, she continued to read or sing in the same soothing tone. About halfway through the session, she took a bin of plastic instruments out of the cupboard and passed it around so the babies could jingle bells or pound on drums or bang sticks together. Of course, the kids had a lot more enthusiasm than talent—his daughter included—and by the time they were finished, Braden could feel a headache brewing.

"That was a great effort today," Cassie told them, and he breathed a grateful sigh of relief that they were done. "I'll see you all next week, and please don't forget the Book & Bake Sale on the fifteenth—any and all donations of gently used books are appreciated."

Despite the class being dismissed, none of the moms seemed to be in a hurry to leave, instead continuing to chat with one another about feeding schedules and diaper rashes and teething woes. Braden just wanted to be gone but Saige had somehow managed to pull off her shoes, forcing him to stay put long enough to untie the laces, put the shoes back on her feet and tie them up again.

While he was preoccupied with this task, the woman who had been seated on his left shifted closer. "I'm Heather Turcotte. And this—" she jiggled the baby in her lap "—is Katie."

"Braden Garrett," he told her, confident that she already knew his daughter.

"You're a brave man to subject yourself to a baby class full of women," she said, then smiled at him.

"I'm only here today because my mom had an appointment."

"That's too bad. It would be nice to have another single parent in the group," she told him. "Most of these women don't have a clue how hard it is to raise a child on their own. Of course, I didn't know, either, until I had Katie. All through my pregnancy, I was so certain that I could handle this. But the idea of a baby is a lot different than the reality."

"That's true," he agreed, only half listening to her as he worked Saige's shoes back onto her feet. Out of the corner of his eye, he saw Cassie talking to one of the other moms and cleaning the instruments with antibacterial wipes, which made him feel a little bit better about the bells that his daughter had been chewing on.

"Of course, it helps that I have a flexible schedule at work," Heather was saying. "As I'm sure you do, considering that your name is on the company letterhead."

"There are benefits to working for a family business," he agreed.

Cassie waved goodbye to the other woman and her baby, then carried the bin of instruments to the cupboard.

"Such as being able to take a little extra time to grab a cup of coffee now?" Heather suggested hopefully.

He forced his attention back to her, inwardly wincing at the hopeful expression on her face. "Sorry, I really do need to get to the office."

She pouted, much like his daughter did when she didn't get what she wanted, but the look wasn't nearly as cute on a grown woman who had a daughter of her own.

"Well, maybe we could get the kids together sometime. A playdate for the little ones—" she winked "—*and* the grown-ups."

"I appreciate the invitation, but my time is really limited these days."

"Oh. Okay." She forced a smile, but he could tell that she was disappointed. "Well, if you change your mind, you know where to find me on Tuesday mornings."

"Yes, I do," he confirmed.

Somehow, while he'd been putting on her shoes, Saige had found his phone and was using it as a chew toy. With a sigh, he pried it from her fingers and wiped it on his trousers. "Are you cutting more teeth, sweetie?"

Her only answer was to shove her fist into her mouth.

He picked her up and she dropped her head onto his shoulder, apparently ready for her nap. He bent his knees carefully to reach the daisy pillow and carried it to the librarian. "Thanks for the loan."

"You're welcome," she said. Then, "I wanted to ask about your mother earlier, but I didn't want you to think I was being nosy."

"What did you want to ask?"

"In the past six months, Ellen hasn't missed a single class—I just wondered if she was okay."

"Oh. Yes, she's fine. At least, I think so," he told her. "She chipped a tooth at breakfast and had an emergency appointment at the dentist."

"Well, please tell her that I hope she's feeling better and I'm looking forward to seeing her on Thursday."

"Is that your way of saying that you don't want to see me on Thursday?" he teased.

"This is a public library, Mr. Garrett," she pointed out. "You're welcome any time the doors are open."

"And will I find you here if I come back?" he wondered.

"Most days," she confirmed.

"So this is your real job—you don't work anywhere else?"

Her brows lifted at that. "Yes, this is my real job," she said, her tone cooler now by several degrees.

And despite having turned down Heather's offer of coffee only a few minutes earlier, he found the prospect of enjoying a hot beverage with this woman an incredibly appealing one. "Can you sneak away for a cup of coffee?"

She seemed surprised by the invitation—and maybe a little tempted—but after a brief hesitation, she shook her head. "No, I can't. I'm working, Mr. Garrett."

"I know," he said, and offered her what he'd been told was a charming smile. "But the class is finished and I'm sure that whatever else you have to do can wait for half an hour or so while we go across the street to the café."

"Obviously you think that 'whatever else' I have to do is pretty insignificant," she noted, her tone downright frosty now.

"I didn't mean to offend you, Miss MacKinnon," he said, because it was obvious that he'd done so.

"I may not be the CEO of a national corporation, but the work I do matters to the people who come here." She moved toward the door where she hit a switch on the wall to turn off the overhead lights—a clear sign that it was time for him to leave.

He stepped out of the room, and she closed and locked the door. "Have a good day, Mr. Garrett."

"I will," he said. "But I need one more thing before I go."

"What's that?" she asked warily.

"A library card."

Cassie stared at him for a moment, trying to decide if he was joking. "*You* want a library card?"

"I assume I need one to borrow books," Braden said matter-of-factly.

"You do," she confirmed, still wondering about his angle—because she was certain that he had one.

"So where do I get a card?" he prompted, sounding sincere in his request.

But how could she know for sure? If her recent experience with the male species had taught her nothing else, she'd at least learned that she wasn't a good judge of their intentions or motivations.

"Follow me," she said.

He did, and with each step, she was conscious of him beside her—not just his presence but his masculinity. The library wasn't a female domain. A lot of males came through the doors every day—mostly boys, a few teens and some older men. Rarely did she cross paths with a male in the twenty-five to forty-four age bracket. Never had she crossed paths with anyone like Braden Garrett.

He was the type of man who made heads turn and hearts flutter and made women think all kinds of naughty thoughts. And his nearness now made her skin feel hot and tight, tingly in a way that made her uneasy. Cassie didn't want to feel tingly, she didn't want to think about how long it had been since she'd been attracted, on a purely physical level, to a man, and she definitely didn't want to be attracted to this man now.

Aside from the fact that he was a Garrett and, therefore, way out of her league, she had no intention of wasting a single minute of her time with a man who didn't value who she was. Not again. Thankfully, his disparaging remark about her job was an effective antidote to his good looks and easy charm.

Taking a seat at the computer, she logged in to create a new account. He took his driver's license out of his wallet so that she could input the necessary data. She noted that his middle name was Michael, his thirty-ninth birthday was coming up and he lived in one of the most exclusive parts of town.

"What kind of books do you like to read?" she inquired, as she would of any other newcomer to the library.

"Mostly historical fiction and nonfiction, some action-thriller type stories."

"Like Bernard Cornwell, Tom Clancy and Clive Cussler?"

He nodded. "And John Jakes and Diana Gabaldon."

She looked up from the computer screen. "You read Diana Gabaldon?"

"Sure," he said, not the least bit self-conscious about the admission. "My cousin, Tristyn, left a copy of *Outlander* at my place on Ocracoke and I got hooked."

For a moment while they'd been chatting about favorite authors, she'd almost let herself believe he was a normal person—just a handsome single dad hanging out at the library with his daughter. But the revelation that he not only lived in Forrest Hill but had another house on an island in the Outer Banks immediately dispelled that notion.

"My brothers tease me about reading romance," he continued, oblivious to her thought process, "but there's a lot more to her books than that."

"There's a lot more to most romance novels than many people believe," she told him.

"What do you like to read?" he asked her.

"Anything and everything," she said. "I have favorite authors, of course, but I try to read across the whole spectrum in order to be able to make recommendations to our patrons." She set his newly printed library card on the counter along with a pen for him to sign it.

He did, then tucked the new card and his identification back into his wallet. By this time, Saige had lost the battle to keep her eyes open, and the image of that sweet little girl sleeping in his arms tugged at something inside of her.

"Congratulations," she said, ignoring the unwelcome tug. "You are now an official card-carrying member of the Charisma Public Library."

"Thank you." He picked up one of the flyers advertising the Book & Bake Sale along with a monthly schedule of classes and activities, then slid both into the side pocket of Saige's diaper bag. "I guess that means I'll be seeing you around."

She nodded, but she didn't really believe him. And as she watched him walk out the door, she assured herself that was for the best. Because the last thing she needed was to be crossing paths with a man who made her feel tingles she didn't want to be feeling.

His daughter slept until Braden got her to the office. As soon as he tried to lay her down, Saige was wide-awake and wanting his attention. He dumped the toys from her diaper bag into the playpen—squishy blocks and finger puppets and board books—so that she could occupy herself while he worked. She decided to invent a new game: throw things at Daddy. Thankfully, she wasn't strong enough to fling the books very far, but after several blocks bounced across the surface of his desk, he decided there was no point in hanging around the office when he obviously wasn't going to get anything accomplished.

There were definite advantages to working in a family business, and since his baby wouldn't be a baby forever, he decided to take the rest of the day off to spend with her. He took her to the indoor play center, where she could jump and climb and swing and burn off all of the energy she seemed to have in abundance. Then, when she was finally tired of all of that, he took her to "Aunt" Rachel's shop—Buds & Blooms—to pick out some flowers, then to his parents' house to see how Ellen had fared at the dentist.

"Ga-ma!" Saige said, flinging herself at her grandmother's legs.

"I didn't think I was going to get to see you today," Ellen said, ruffling her granddaughter's silky black hair. "And I was missing you."

"I'm sure she missed you more," Braden said, handing the bouquet to his mother. "She was not a happy camper at the office today."

"Offices aren't fun places for little ones." Ellen brought the flowers closer to her nose and inhaled their fragrant scent. "These are beautiful—what's the occasion?"

"No occasion—I just realized that I take for granted how much you do for me and Saige every day and wanted to show our appreciation," he told her. "But now that I see the swelling of your jaw, I'm thinking they might be 'get well' flowers—what did the dentist do to you?"

"He extracted the tooth."

"I thought it was only a chip."

"So did I," she admitted, lowering herself into a chair, which Saige interpreted as an invitation to crawl into her lap. "Apparently the chip caused a crack that went all the way down to the root, so they had to take it out."

He winced instinctively.

"Now I have to decide whether I want a bridge or an implant."

"And I'll bet you're wishing you had oatmeal instead of granola for breakfast," he noted, filling a vase with water for her flowers.

"It will definitely be oatmeal tomorrow," she said. "How was Baby Talk?"

"Fine," he said, "aside from the fact that I was the only man in a room full of women, apparently all of whom know my life story."

"They don't know your whole life story," his mother denied.

"How much do they know?"

"I might have mentioned that you're a single father."

"Might have mentioned?" he echoed suspiciously.

"Well, in a group of much younger women, it was immediately apparent that Saige isn't my child. Someone— I think it was Annalise—asked if I looked after her while her mother was at work and I said no, that I looked after her while her dad's at work because Saige doesn't have a mother."

"Hmm," he said. He couldn't fault his mother for answering the question, but he didn't like the way she made him sound like some kind of "super dad" just because he was taking care of his daughter—especially when they both knew there was no way he'd be able to manage without Ellen's help.

"And you're not the only single parent with a child in the group," she pointed out. "There are a couple of single moms there, too."

"I met Heather," he admitted.

"She's a pretty girl. And a loving mother."

"I'm not interested in a woman who's obviously looking for a man to be a father to her child," he warned.

"She told you that?"

"She gave me the 'single parenthood is so much harder than most people realize' speech."

"Which you already know," she pointed out.

He nodded again.

"So maybe you should think about finding a new mother for Saige," she urged.

"Because the third time's the charm?" he asked skeptically.

"Because a little girl needs a mother," she said firmly. "And because you deserve to have someone in your life, too."

"I have Saige," he reminded her, as he always did when she started in on this particular topic. But this time the automatic response was followed by a picture of the pretty librarian forming in his mind.

"And no one doubts how much you love her," Ellen acknowledged. "But if you do your job as a parent right— and I expect you will—she's going to grow up and go off to live her own life one day, and then who will you have?"

"I think I've got a few years before I need to worry about that," he pointed out. "And maybe by then, I'll be ready to start dating again."

His mother's sigh was filled with resignation.

"By the way," he said, in a desperate effort to shift the topic of conversation away from his blank social calendar, "Cassie said that she hopes you feel better soon."

As soon as he mentioned the librarian's name, a speculative gleam sparked in his mother's eyes that warned his effort had been for naught.

"She's such a sweet girl," Ellen said. "Smart and beautiful, and so ideally suited for her job."

Braden had intended to keep his mouth firmly shut, not wanting to be drawn into a discussion about Miss Mac-Kinnon's many attributes. But the last part of his mother's statement piqued his curiosity. "She's a librarian—what kind of qualifications does she need?"

His mother frowned her disapproval. "The janitor who scrubs the floors of a surgery is just as crucial as the doctor who performs the operation," she reminded him.

"But she's not a surgeon or a janitor," he pointed out. "She's a librarian." And he didn't think keeping a collection of books in order required any particular knowledge outside of the twenty-six letters of the alphabet.

"With a master's degree in library studies."

"I didn't know there was such a discipline," he acknowledged.

"Apparently there are a lot of things you don't know," she said pointedly.

He nodded an acknowledgment of the fact. "I guess, when I went into the library, I was expecting to find someone more like Miss Houlahan behind the desk."

His mother chuckled. "Irene Houlahan's been retired more than half a dozen years now."

"I'm relieved to know she's no longer terrifying young book borrowers."

"She wasn't terrifying," Ellen chided. "You were only afraid of her because you lost a library book."

"I didn't lose it," he denied. "I just couldn't find it when it was due. And you made me pay the late fines out of my allowance."

"Because you were the one who misplaced it," she pointed out logically.

"That's probably why I buy my books now—I'd rather pay for them up front and without guilt."

Which didn't begin to explain why he was now carrying a library card in his wallet—or his determination to put it to use in the near future.

Chapter Three

Cassie stood with her back against the counter as she lifted the last forkful of cheesy macaroni to her mouth.

"You might be surprised to hear that I like to cook," she said to Westley and Buttercup. "I just don't do it very often because it's not worth the effort to prepare a whole meal for one person."

Aside from the crunch of the two cats chowing down on their seafood medley, there was no response.

"Maybe I should get a dog," she mused. "Dogs at least wag their tails when you talk to them."

As usual, the two strays she'd rescued from a box in the library parking lot ignored her.

"Unfortunately, a dog would be a lot less tolerant of the occasional ten-hour shift at the library," she noted.

That was one good thing about Westley and Buttercup— they didn't really need her except when their food or water bowls were empty. And when she was away for several hours at a time, she didn't worry because they had one another for company.

But she did worry that she was turning into a cliché—the lonely librarian with only her cats and her books to keep her company. Since Westley and Buttercup were more interested in their dinner than the woman who fed it to them, she put her bowl and spoon in the dishwasher, then went into the living room and turned her attention to the tightly packed shelves.

The books were her reliable companions and steadfast friends. She had other friends, of course—real people that she went to the movies with or met for the occasional cup of coffee. But most of her friends were married now, with husbands and children to care for. It wasn't that Cassie didn't want to fall in love, get married and have a family, but she was beginning to wonder if it would ever happen. The few serious relationships she'd had in the past had all ended with her heart—if not broken—at least battered and bruised. When she'd met Joel Langdon three years earlier, she'd thought he was finally the one. Three months after he'd put a ring on her finger, she'd realized that her judgment was obviously faulty.

Thankfully, she was usually content with her own company. And when she wasn't, she could curl up with Captain Brandon Birmingham or Dean Robillard or Roarke. But tonight, she reached out a hand and plucked a random book from the shelf. A smile curved her lips when she recognized the cover of a beloved Jennifer Crusie novel.

She made herself a cup of tea and settled into her favorite chair by the fireplace, happy to lose herself in the story and fall in love with Cal as Min did. But who wouldn't love a man who appreciated her shoe collection, fed her doughnuts and didn't want to change a single thing about her? All of that, and he was great in bed, too.

She sighed and set the book aside to return her empty mug to the kitchen. Of course Cal was perfect—he was fictional. And she wasn't looking for perfect, anyway— she just wanted to meet a man who would appreciate her for who she was without trying to make her into someone different. He didn't have to be mouthwateringly gorgeous or Rhodes Scholar smart, but he had to be kind to children and animals and have a good relationship with his family. And it would be a definite plus if she felt flutters in her tummy when he smiled at her.

As she pieced together the ideal qualities in her mind, a picture began to form—a picture that looked very much like Braden Garrett.

Braden planned to wait a week or so before he tried out his library card to avoid appearing too eager. He figured seven to ten days was a reasonable time frame, and then, if he saw Cassie again and had the same immediate and visceral reaction, he would consider his next move.

He'd been widowed for just over a year and married for six years prior to that, so it had been a long time since he'd made any moves. How much had the dating scene changed in those years? Were any of the moves the same? Was he ready to start dating again and risk jeopardizing the precious relationship he had with his daughter by bringing someone new into their lives?

Except that Cassie was already in Saige's life—or at least on the periphery of it. And by all accounts, his little girl was enamored of the librarian. After only one brief meeting, he'd found himself aware of her appeal. Which was just one reason he'd decided to take a step back and give his suddenly reawakened hormones a chance to cool down.

But when he picked up his daughter's clothes to dump

them into the laundry basket, he found the red engine that she'd been reluctant to let go of at the train table earlier that day. He had a clear memory of prying the toy from her clenched fist and setting it back on the track, but apparently—maybe when he turned his back to retrieve her diaper bag—his daughter had picked it up again.

Wednesday morning he dropped Saige off at his parents' house, then headed toward his office as usual. But, conscious of the little red engine in his pocket, he detoured toward the library on his way. He'd considered leaving the train with his mother so that she could return it, but the "borrowed" toy was the perfect excuse for him to see the pretty librarian again and he was going to take advantage of it.

For the first six months after Dana's death, his mother hadn't pushed him outside of his comfort zone. Ellen understood that he was grieving for his wife and adjusting to his role as a new—and now single—dad. But since Christmas, she'd started to hint that it was time for him to move on with his life and urged him to get out and meet new people. More recently, she'd made it clear that when she said "people" she meant "women."

He knew she was motivated by concern—that she didn't want him to be alone. But whenever he dared to remind her that he wasn't alone because he had his daughter, she pointed out that Saige needed a mother. Saige deserved a mother. And that was a truth Braden could not dispute.

A real home with two parents.

He shook off the echo of those words and the guilt that weighed on his heart. He wasn't interested in getting involved with anyone right now. He had neither the time nor the energy to invest in a romantic relationship.

Getting some action between the sheets, on the other hand, held some definite appeal. But he knew that if he was just looking for sex, he should not be looking at the local librarian. Especially not when the woman was obviously adored by both his mother and his daughter.

But if he took the train back to the library, well, that was simply the right thing to do. And if he happened to see Cassie MacKinnon while he was there, that would just be a lucky coincidence.

Cassie didn't expect to ever see Braden again.

Despite his request for a library card, she didn't think he would actually use it. Men like Braden Garrett didn't borrow anything—if he wanted something he didn't have, he would buy it. And considering how busy the CEO and single father must be, she didn't imagine that he had much free time to read anything aside from business reports.

All of which made perfect, logical sense. What didn't make any sense at all was that she found herself thinking about him anyway, and wishing he would walk through the front doors in contradiction of her logic.

She tried to push these thoughts from her mind, annoyed by her inexplicable preoccupation with a man she was undeniably attracted to but wasn't sure she liked very much. A man who wasn't so very different from any other member of the male species who came through the library.

Okay, that was a lie. The truth was, she'd never met anyone else quite like Braden Garrett. But there were a lot of other guys in the world—good-looking, intelligent and charming guys. Some of them even came into the library and flirted with her and didn't regard her job as inconsequential. Rarely did she ever think about any of them after they were gone; never did she dream about any of them.

Until last night.

What was wrong with her? Why was she so captivated by a guy she'd met only once? A man who wasn't only gor-

geous and rich but a single father undoubtedly still grieving for the wife he'd lost only a year earlier.

Because even if he was interested in her, and even if it
turned out that he wasn't as shallow and judgmental as her
initial impressions indicated him to be, she had no intention
of getting involved with a man who was still in love with
another woman. No way. She'd been there, done that already, and she still had the bruises on her heart to prove it.

So it was a good thing she would probably never see
Braden Garrett again. A very good thing.

Or so she thought until she glanced up to offer assis-
tance to the patron who had stopped at her desk—and
found herself looking at the subject of her preoccupation.

Her heart skipped a beat and then raced to catch up. She
managed a smile, determined not to let him know how he
affected her. "Good morning, Mr. Garrett. Are you looking for some reading material today?"

He shook his head. "Returning some smuggled mer-
chandise." He set a red engine on top of her desk. "Apparently Saige loves the trains more than I realized."

It wasn't the first toy to go missing from the playroom,
and she knew it wouldn't be the last. Thankfully, the "borrowed" items were usually returned by the embarrassed
parents of the pint-size pickpockets when they were found.

"Universal toddler rules," she acknowledged. "If it's in
my hand, it's mine."

"Sounds like the kind of wisdom that comes from experience," he noted, his gaze shifting to her left hand. "Do
you have kids?"

She shook her head and ignored the emptiness she felt
inside whenever she thought about the family she might
have had by now if she'd married Joel instead of giving
him back his ring. "No," she said lightly. "But I've spent
enough time in the children's section to have learned a lot."

"What about a husband?" he prompted. "Fiancé? Boyfriend?"

No, no and *no.* But she kept those responses to herself, saying only, "Thank you for returning the train, Mr. Garrett."

"I'll interpret that as a no," he said, with just the hint of a smile curving his lips.

And even that hint was potent enough to make her knees weak, which irritated her beyond reason. "You should interpret it as none of your business," she told him.

Her blunt response had no effect on his smile. "Except that if you'd had a husband, fiancé or boyfriend, you would have said so," he pointed out reasonably. "And since there's no husband, fiancé or boyfriend, maybe you'll let me buy you a cup of coffee and apologize for whatever I did that put your back up."

Before she could think of a response to that, Megan hurried up to the desk. "I'm sorry I got caught up with Mrs. Lynch and made you late for your break, Cassie."

"That's okay," she said. "I wanted to finish logging these new books into the system before I left the desk."

"I can do that," her coworker offered helpfully.

Cassie thanked Megan, though she was feeling anything but grateful. Because as much as she was desperate for a hit of caffeine, she suspected that Braden would tag along on her break and his presence would make her jittery for a different reason.

"I guess you're free for that coffee, then?" he prompted.

"I'm going across the street for my break," she confirmed, unlocking the bottom drawer of the desk to retrieve her purse. "And while I may not be a corporate executive, I can afford to buy my own coffee."

"I'm sure you can," he agreed. "But if I pay for it, you might feel obligated to sit down with me to drink it."

And apparently her determination to remain unaffected was no match for his effortless charm, because she felt a smile tug at her own lips as she replied, "Only if there's a brownie with the coffee."

Growing up a Garrett in Charisma, Braden wasn't accustomed to having to work so hard for a woman's attention. And while he was curious about the reasons for Cassie's reluctance to spend time with him, he decided to save the questions for later.

He pulled open the door of the Bean There Café and gestured for her to precede him. There were a few customers in line ahead of them at the counter, allowing him to peruse the pastry offerings in the display case while they waited. He ordered a lemon poppy-seed muffin and a large coffee, black; Cassie opted for a salted caramel brownie and a vanilla latte.

"How's this?" he asked, gesturing to a couple of leather armchairs close together on one side of the fireplace, further isolated by a display of gift sets on the opposite side of the seating.

"Looks…cozy," she said.

He grinned. "Too cozy?"

She narrowed her gaze, but he suspected that she wouldn't turn away from the challenge. A suspicion that was proven correct when she sat in the chair closest to the fire.

The flickering flames provided light and warmth and the soft, comfy seating around the perimeter of the room provided a much more intimate atmosphere than the straight-back wooden chairs and square tables in the center. Braden relaxed into the leather seat beside Cassie and set his muffin on the small table between them.

"Are you going to let me apologize now?" he asked her.

She eyed him over the rim of her cup as she sipped. "What are you apologizing for?"

"Whatever I said or did to offend you."

"You don't even know, do you?" she asked, her tone a combination of amusement and exasperation.

"I'm afraid to guess," he admitted. But he did know it had happened the previous morning, sometime after Baby Talk, because her demeanor toward him had shifted from warm to cool in about two seconds.

She shook her head and broke off a corner of her brownie. "It doesn't matter."

"If it didn't matter, you wouldn't still be mad," he pointed out.

"I'm not still mad."

He lifted his brows.

"Okay, I'm still a little bit mad," she acknowledged. "But it's not really your fault—you didn't do anything but speak out loud the same thoughts that too many people have about my work."

"I'm still confused," he admitted. "What did I say?"

"You asked if working at the library was my real job."

He winced. "I assure you the question was more a reflection of my interest in learning about you than an opinion of your work," he said. "And probably influenced by a lack of knowledge about what a librarian actually does."

"My responsibilities are various and endless."

"I'll admit, I was surprised to see so many people at the library yesterday. I figured most everyone did their research and reading on their own tablets or computers these days."

"To paraphrase Neil Gaiman, an internet search engine can find a hundred thousand answers—a librarian can help you find the right one."

"My mother's a big fan of his work," Braden noted.

"I know," she admitted. "Anytime we get a new book with his name on it, I put it aside for her."

"She's a fan of yours, too," he said.

Her lips curved, and he felt that tug low in his belly again. There was just something about her smile—an innocent sensuality that got to him every time and made him want to be the reason for her happiness.

"Because I put aside the books she wants," Cassie said again.

"I think there's more to it than that," he remarked. "How long have you known her?"

"As long as I've worked at CPL, which is twelve years."

"Really?" He didn't know if he was more surprised to learn that she'd worked at the library for so many years or that she'd known his mother for that amount of time.

"I started as a volunteer when I was still in high school," she explained. "And in addition to being an avid reader, Ellen is one of the volunteers who delivers books to patrons who are unable to get to the library."

"I didn't know that," he admitted. "Between the Acquisitions Committee of the Art Gallery, the Board of Directors at Mercy Hospital and, for the past year, taking care of Saige three to five days a week for me, I wouldn't have thought she'd have time for anything else."

"She obviously likes to keep busy," Cassie noted. "And I know how much she adores her grandchildren. Ever since Ryan and Harper got custody of little Oliver almost three years ago, I've seen new pictures almost every week.

"Of course, hundreds of pictures when Vanessa was born, and hundreds more when Saige was born," she continued. "And I know she's overjoyed that Ryan and Harper are moving back to Charisma—hopefully before their second child is born."

"You're probably more up-to-date on my family than I

am," he admitted. "I don't even know my sister-in-law's due date."

"August twenty-eighth."

"Which proves my point." He polished off the last bite of his muffin.

She broke off another piece of brownie and popped it into her mouth. Then she licked a smear of caramel off her thumb—a quick and spontaneous swipe of her tongue over her skin that probably wasn't intended to be provocative but certainly had that effect on his body and thoughts.

"I only remember the date because it happens to be my birthday, too," she admitted.

He sipped his coffee. "As a librarian, how much do you know about chemistry?"

"Enough to pass the course in high school." She smiled. "Barely."

"And what do you think we should do about this chemistry between us?" he asked.

She choked on her latte. "Excuse me?"

"I'm stumbling here," he acknowledged. "Because it's been a long time since I've been attracted to a woman—other than my wife, I mean."

She eyed him warily. "Are you saying that you're attracted to me?"

"Why else would I be here when there are at least a dozen coffee shops closer to my office?"

"I thought you came to the library to return the train Saige took home."

"That was my excuse to come by and see you," he said.

She dropped her gaze to her plate, using her fingertip to push the brownie crumbs into the center.

"You didn't expect me to admit that, did you?"

"I didn't expect it to be true," she told him.

"I was a little surprised myself," he confided. "When I

found the train, I planned to leave it with my mother, for her to return. And when I dropped Saige off this morning, I had it with me, but for some reason, I held on to it. As I headed toward my office, I figured I'd give it to her later. Except that I couldn't stop thinking about you."

She wiped her fingers on her napkin, then folded it on top of her plate.

"This would be a good time for you to admit that you've been thinking about me, too," he told her.

"Even if it's not true?"

He reached across the table and stroked a finger over the back of her hand. She went immediately and completely still, not even breathing as her gaze locked with his.

"You've thought about me," he said. "Whether you're willing to admit it or not."

"Maybe I have," she acknowledged, slowly pulling her hand away. "Once or twice."

"So what do you think we should do about this chemistry?" he asked again.

"I'm the wrong person to ask," she said lightly. "All of my experiments simply fizzled and died."

"Maybe you were working with the wrong partner," he suggested.

"Maybe." She finished her latte and set the mug on top of her empty plate. "I really need to get back to work, but thanks for the coffee and the brownie."

"Anytime."

He stayed where he was and watched her walk away, because he'd never in his life chased after a woman and he wasn't going to start now.

Instead, he took his time finishing his coffee before he headed back to his own office—where he thought of her throughout the rest of the day, because he knew he would be seeing the sexy librarian again. Very soon.

Chapter Four

When Cassie left work later that afternoon, she headed to Serenity Gardens to visit Irene Houlahan. Almost three years earlier, the former librarian had slipped and fallen down her basement stairs, a nasty tumble that resulted in a broken collarbone and femur and forced her to sell her two-story home and move into the assisted-living facility for seniors.

The septuagenarian had never married, had no children and no family in Charisma, but once upon a time, she'd changed Cassie's life. No, she'd done more than change her life—she'd saved it. And Cassie knew that she'd never be able to repay the woman who was so much more to her than a friend and mentor.

Since Irene had taken up residence at Serenity Gardens, Cassie had visited her two or three times a week. The move had been good for Irene, who was now surrounded by contemporaries who encouraged her to take part in various social activities on the property. And then, just after the New Year, Jerry Riordan had moved in across the hall.

His arrival had generated a fair amount of buzz among the residents and staff, and Cassie had overheard enough to know that he was seventy-two years old, a retired civil engineer and widower with three children and eight grandchildren, all of whom lived out of state. He was close to six feet tall, slender of build and apparently in possession of all of his own teeth, which made him the object of much female admiration within the residence.

But far more interesting to Cassie was her discovery that the newest resident of the fifth floor was spending a fair amount of time with the retired librarian. One day when Cassie was visiting, she'd asked Irene about her history with Jerry. Her friend had ignored the question, instead instructing Cassie to find *To Kill a Mockingbird* on her shelf. Of course, the woman's personal library was as ruthlessly organized as the public facility, so Cassie found it easily—an old and obviously much-read volume with a dust jacket curling at the edges.

"You've obviously had this a very long time."

"A lot more years than you've been alive," Irene acknowledged.

Cassie opened the cover to check the copyright page, but her attention was caught by writing inside the front cover. Knowing that her friend would never deface a work of art—and books undoubtedly fit that description—the bold strokes of ink snagged her attention.

Irene held out her hand. "The book."

The impatience in her tone didn't stop Cassie from taking a quick peek at the inscription:

To Irene—who embodies all the best characteristics of Scout, Jem and Dill. One day you will be the

*heroine of your own adventures, but for now, I hope
you enjoy their story.
Happy Birthday,
Jerry*

She closed the cover and looked at her friend. "Jerry—as in Jerry Riordan?"

"Did someone mention my name?" the man asked from the doorway.

"Were your ears burning?" Irene snapped at him.

Jerry shrugged. "Might have been—my hearing's not quite what it used to be." Then he spotted the volume in Cassie's hand and his pale blue eyes lit up. "Well, that book is familiar."

"There are more than thirty million copies of it in print," Irene pointed out.

"And that looks like the same copy I gave to you for your fourteenth birthday," he said.

"Probably because it is," she acknowledged, finally abandoning any pretense of faulty memory.

"I can't believe you still have it," Jerry said, speaking so softly it was almost as if he was talking to himself.

"It's one of my favorite books," she said. "Why would I get rid of it?"

"Over the years, things have a tendency to go missing or be forgotten."

"Maybe by some people," the old woman said pointedly.

"I never forgot you, Irene," Jerry assured her.

Cassie continued to stand beside the bookcase, wondering if she was actually invisible or just felt that way. She didn't mind being ignored and she had no intention of interrupting what was—judging by the unfamiliar flush in her friend's usually pale cheeks—a deeply personal moment.

Years ago, when Cassie had asked Irene why she'd never

married, the older woman had snapped that it wasn't a conscious choice to be alone—that sometimes the right man found the right woman in someone else. Of course, Cassie hadn't known what she meant at the time, and Irene had refused to answer any more questions on the subject. Watching her friend with Jerry now, she thought she finally understood.

"Are you going to sit down and read the book or just stand there?" Irene finally asked her.

Cassie knew her too well to be offended by the brusque tone. "I was just waiting for the two of you to finish your stroll down memory lane," she responded lightly.

"I don't stroll anywhere with six pins in my leg and I wouldn't stroll with him even if I could," Irene said primly.

"Thankfully, it's just your leg and not your arms that are weak," Jerry teased. "Otherwise you'd have trouble holding on to that grudge."

Cassie fought against a smile as she settled back into a wing chair, turned to the first page and began reading while Jerry lowered himself onto the opposite end of the sofa from Irene.

She read three chapters before she was interrupted by voices in the hall as the residents started to make their way to the activity room for Beach Party Bingo. Irene professed to despise bingo but she was fond of the fruit skewers and virgin coladas they served to go with the beach party theme.

When Cassie glanced up, she noted that Jerry had shifted on the sofa so that he was sitting closer to Irene now. Not so close that she could find his ribs with a sharp elbow if the mood struck her to do so, but definitely much closer. Apparently the man still had some moves—and he was making them on her friend.

"I think that's a good place to stop for today," she decided, sliding a bookmark between the pages.

"Thank you for the visit," Irene said, as she always did.

Cassie, too, gave her usual response. "It was my pleasure."

She set the book down on the coffee table, then touched her lips to her friend's soft, wrinkled cheek.

Irene waved her away, uncomfortable with the display of affection.

"What about me?" Jerry said, tapping his cheek with an arthritic finger. "I'd never wave off a kiss from a pretty girl."

"Isn't that the truth?" Irene muttered under her breath.

Cassie kissed his cheek, too. "Good night, Mr. Riordan. I'll see you on Friday, Irene."

"There's a trip to Noah's Landing on Friday," her friend said. "We're not scheduled to be back until dinnertime."

"Then I'll come Friday night," Cassie offered.

"That's fine."

"No, it's not," Jerry protested. "You can't ask a beautiful young woman to spend her Friday night hanging out with a bunch of grumpy old folks."

"I didn't ask, Cassandra offered," Irene pointed out. "And she comes to visit *me*, not any other grumpy old folks who decide to wander into my room uninvited."

"Well, I'm sure Cassandra has better things to do on a Friday night," he said, glancing at Cassie expectantly.

"Actually, I don't have any plans," she admitted.

He scowled. "You don't have a date?"

She shook her head.

"What's wrong with the young men in this town?" Jerry wondered.

"They're as shortsighted and thickheaded now as they were fifty years ago," Irene told him.

"And on that note," Cassie said, inching toward the door.

"I'll see you in a few days," Irene said.

"Don't come on Friday," Jerry called out to her. "I'm going to keep Irene busy at the cribbage board."

"I have cataracts," she protested.

"And I have a deck of cards with large print numbers."

Cassie left them bickering, happy to know that her friend had a new beau to fill some of her quiet hours. And eager to believe that if romance was in the air for Irene, maybe it wasn't too late for her, either.

Of course, if she wanted to fall in love, she'd have to be willing to open up her heart again, and that was a step she wasn't sure she was ready to take. Because what she'd told Braden about her struggles with chemistry was only partly true. About half of her experiments had fizzled into nothingness—the other half had flared so bright and hot, she'd ended up getting burned. And she simply wasn't willing to play with fire again.

While Braden wouldn't trade his baby girl for anything in the world, there were times when he would willingly sacrifice a limb for eight consecutive hours of sleep.

"Come on, Saige," he said wearily. "It's two a.m. That's not play time—it's sleep time."

"Wound an' wound," she said, clapping her hands.

He reached into her crib for her favorite toy—a stuffed sock monkey that had been a gift from her birth mother—and gave it to Saige. "Sleep. Sleep. Sleep."

She immediately grabbed the monkey's arm and cuddled it close. Then she tipped her head back to look at him, and when she smiled, he gave in with a sigh. "You know just how to wrap me around your finger, don't you?"

"Da-da," she said.

He touched his lips to the top of her head, breathing in the familiar scent of her baby shampoo.

She was the baby he and Dana had been wanting for most of their six-year marriage, the child they'd almost given up hope of ever having. In the last few weeks leading up to her birth, they'd finally, cautiously, started to transform one of the spare bedrooms into a nursery. They'd hung a mobile over the crib, put tiny little onesies and sleepers in the dresser, and stocked up on diapers and formula.

At the same time, they'd both been a little hesitant to believe that this time, finally, their dream of having a child would come true. Because they were aware that the birth mother could decide, at the last minute, to keep her baby. And they knew that, if she did, they couldn't blame her.

But Lindsay Benson had been adamant. She wanted a better life for her baby than to be raised by a single mother who hadn't yet graduated from college. She wanted her daughter to have a real family with two parents who would care for her and love her and who could afford to give her not just the necessities of life but some extras, too.

Within a few weeks, Braden had begun to suspect that he and Dana wouldn't be that family. For some reason that he couldn't begin to fathom—or maybe didn't want to admit—his wife wasn't able to bond with the baby. Every time Saige cried, Dana pushed the baby at him, claiming that she had a headache. Every time Saige needed a bottle or diaper change, Dana was busy doing something else. Every time Saige woke up in the middle of the night, Dana pretended not to hear her.

Yes, he'd seen the signs, but he'd still been optimistic that she would come around. That she just needed some more time. She'd suffered so much disappointment over the years, he was certain it was her lingering fear of losing the child they'd wanted so much that was holding her back. He refused to consider that Dana might be unhappy because their adopted daughter was so obviously not their biological child.

Then, when Saige was six weeks old, Dana made her big announcement: she didn't really want to be a mother or a wife. She told him that she'd found an apartment and would be moving out at the end of March. Oh, and she needed a check to cover first and last month's rent.

And Braden, fool that he was, gave it to her. Because they'd been married for six years and he honestly hoped that the separation would only be a temporary measure, that after a few months—or hopefully even sooner—she would want to come home to her husband and daughter. Except that a few weeks later, she'd died when her car was T-boned by a semi that blew through a red light.

He hadn't told anyone that Dana was planning to leave him. He'd been blindsided by the announcement, embarrassed that he hadn't been able to hold his marriage together. As a result, while his family tried to be supportive, no one could possibly understand how complicated and convoluted his emotions were.

He did grieve—for the life he'd imagined they might have together, and for his daughter, who had lost another mother. But he was also grateful that he had Saige—her innocent smile and joyful laugh were the sunshine in his days.

If he had any regrets, it was that his little girl didn't have a mother. Her own had given her up so that she could have a real family with two parents. That dream hadn't even lasted three months. Now it was just the two of them.

"Well, the two of us and about a thousand other Garretts," he said to his little girl. "And everyone loves you, so maybe I should stop worrying that you don't have a Mommy."

"Ma-ma," Saige said.

And despite Braden's recent assertion, he sighed. "You've been listening to your grandma, haven't you?"

"Ga-ma."

"You'll see Grandma tomorrow—no," he amended, glancing at his watch. "In just a few hours now."

She smiled again.

"And I bet you'll have another three-hour nap for her, won't you?"

"Choo-choo."

"After she takes you to the library to play with the trains," he confirmed.

She clapped her hands together again, clearly thrilled with his responses to her questions.

Of course, thinking about the library made him think about Cassie. And thinking about Cassie made him want Cassie.

The physical attraction was unexpected but not unwelcome. If anything, his feelings for the librarian reassured him that, despite being a widower and single father, he was still a man with the usual wants and needs.

Unfortunately, Cassie didn't seem like the kind of woman to indulge in a no-strings affair, and he wasn't prepared to offer any more than that.

Cassie had updated the bulletin board in the children's section to suggest Spring into a Good Book and was pinning cardboard flowers to the board when Stacey found her.

"I've been looking all over for you," her friend and coworker said.

"Is there a problem?"

"Nothing aside from the fact that I'm dying to hear all of the details about your hottie," Stacey admitted.

"Who?"

"Don't play that game with me," the other woman chided. "Megan told me you went for coffee with a new guy yesterday."

Cassie acknowledged that with a short nod. "Braden Garrett."

"As in the Garrett Furniture Garretts?"

She nodded.

"Not just hot but rich," Stacey noted. "Does this mean you've decided to end your dating hiatus?"

"Not with Braden Garrett," she said firmly.

"Because hot and rich men aren't your type?" her friend asked, disbelief evident in her tone.

"Because arrogant and insulting men aren't my type," Cassie clarified, as she added some fluffy white clouds to the blue sky.

"Which button of yours did he push?" Stacey asked, absently rubbing a hand over her pregnant belly.

"He asked if this was my real job."

"Ouch. Okay, so he's an idiot," her coworker agreed. "But still—" she held out her hands as if balancing scales "—a hot and rich idiot."

"And then he apologized," she admitted.

"So points for that," Stacey said.

"Maybe," Cassie allowed. "He also told me he's attracted to me."

"Gotta love a guy who tells it like it is."

"Maybe," she said again.

Stacey frowned at her noncommittal response. "Are you not attracted to him?"

"A woman would have to be dead not to be attracted to

him," she acknowledged. "But he's also a widower with a child."

"And you love kids," her friend noted.

"I do." And it was her deepest desire to be a mother someday. "But I don't want to get involved in another relationship with someone who might not actually be interested in me but is only looking for a substitute wife."

"You're not going to be any kind of wife if you don't start dating again," Stacey pointed out to her.

"I'm not opposed to dating," she denied. "I'm just not going to date Braden Garrett."

"How about my cute new neighbor?" her friend suggested. "He's a manager at The Sleep Inn, recently transferred back to Charisma after working the last three years in San Diego."

Cassie shook her head. "You know I don't do blind dates."

"In the past two years, you've hardly had *any* dates," Stacey pointed out. "You need to move on with your life."

She looked at her friend, at the enormous baby bump beneath her pale blue maternity top, and felt a familiar pang of longing. She was sincerely happy for Stacey and her husband who, after several years and numerous fertility treatments, were finally expecting a child, but she couldn't deny that her friend's pregnancy was a daily reminder that her own biological clock was ticking. "You're right," she finally agreed.

"So I can give your number to Darius?"

"Why not?" she decided, and left her friend grinning as she headed upstairs.

Toddler Time was scheduled to start at 10:00 a.m. on Thursdays. By nine fifty, almost all of the usual group were assembled, but Saige wasn't there yet. Cassie found herself watching the clock, wondering if she was going to show and, if she did, whether it would be her father or grandmother who showed up with her.

At nine fifty-seven, Ellen Garrett entered the room with the little girl. Cassie was happy to see the both of them—and maybe just a tiny bit disappointed, too.

The older woman's jaw still looked a little swollen and bruised, but she insisted that she was feeling fine. They didn't have time for more than that basic exchange of pleasantries before the class was scheduled to begin, and Cassie didn't dare delay because she could tell the children were already growing impatient. When the half hour was up, she noticed that Ellen didn't linger as she sometimes did. Instead, she hastily packed up her granddaughter's belongings, said something about errands they needed to run, then disappeared out the door.

It was only after everyone had gone and Cassie was tidying up the room that she discovered Saige Garrett's sock monkey under a table by the windows.

Chapter Five

Braden was just about to leave the office at the end of the day when his mother called.

"I need you to do me a favor," Ellen said.

"Of course," he agreed. Considering everything that his mother did for him, it never occurred to him to refuse her request.

"I can't find Saige's sock monkey. I think she might have left it at story time today."

His daughter never released her viselike grip on her favorite stuffed toy, which made him suspect that Saige hadn't *accidentally* left the monkey anywhere. "And you want me to go by the library to see if it's there," he guessed.

"Well, it is on your way from the office."

"Not really," he pointed out.

"If it's too inconvenient, I can get it tomorrow," Ellen said. "But you'll be the one trying to get Saige to sleep without it tonight."

Unfortunately, that was true. His daughter was rarely without the monkey—and she never went to sleep without it. Still, he could see what his mother was doing. She obviously liked Cassie MacKinnon and was trying to put the pretty librarian in his path as much as possible. And Braden didn't have any objection, really, but he suspected that Cassie might not appreciate his mother's maneuverings.

So he would stop by the library, per his mother's request, and apologize to Cassie for the situation. He would admit that Ellen was probably attempting to do a little matchmaking and suggest that maybe they should have dinner sometime, just to appease her.

Cassie might try to refuse, but he knew she liked his mother and he wasn't opposed to working that angle. In fact, he had the whole scenario worked out in his mind when he walked into the library just after five o'clock. He recognized the woman at the desk as the one who had nudged Cassie along to her coffee break. Megan, if he remembered correctly. He smiled at her. "Hi. I'm looking for Miss MacKinnon."

"I'm sorry, she isn't here right now," Megan told him.

"Oh." He felt a surprisingly sharp pang of disappointment, as if he hadn't realized how much he was looking forward to seeing her again until he was there and she wasn't.

"Is there something I can help you with?" she offered.

"I hope so," he said, because he did have a legitimate reason for this detour. "My daughter, Saige, was here for Toddler Time today and—"

"The sock monkey," Megan realized.

He nodded.

She pulled a clear zipper-seal bag out from under the

desk. Saige's name had been written on the bag with black marker, and her favorite soft toy was inside.

"That's it," he confirmed. "Now we'll both be able to get some sleep tonight."

She smiled. "Is there anything else I can help you with?"

"Can you tell me if Miss MacKinnon is working tomorrow?"

Megan shook her head. "I can't give out that kind of information." Then she sent him a conspiratorial wink. "But if you were to stop by around this time tomorrow, she might be able to tell you herself."

Braden smiled. "Thanks, I just might do that."

At first when Cassie put the phone to her ear and heard the deep masculine voice on the line, her pulse stuttered. When the caller identified himself as Darius Richmond, she experienced a twinge of regret followed by a brief moment of confusion as she tried to place the name.

"Stacey's neighbor," he clarified, and the conversation with her coworker immediately came back to her.

"Of course," she said, mentally chastising herself for thinking—and hoping—that it might have been Braden calling.

"I'm sorry it's taken me so long to call," he apologized. "Stacey gave me your number last week but I've been tied up in meetings with my staff."

"Understandable," she said. "Settling into a new job is always a challenge."

"But I'm free tonight and I'd really like to have dinner with you."

"Tonight," she echoed, her brain scrambling for a valid reason to decline. Then she remembered why she'd agreed to let Stacey give him her number: because she was trying to move on with her life. Because she'd only been out on a handful of dates since breaking up with Joel, and staying home and thinking about Braden Garrett—who, judging by his absence from the library for the past eight days, obviously wasn't thinking about her—wasn't going to help her move on.

"I know it's short notice," he said.

"Actually, tonight is fine," Cassie told him, determined not just to go out but to have a fabulous time.

"Seven o'clock at Valentino's?" he suggested.

"Perfect," she agreed, mentally giving him extra points for his restaurant selection. "I'll see you then."

Cassie disconnected the call and set her phone aside. As much as setups made her nervous, her friend and co-worker was right; she wasn't ever going to find her real-life happily-ever-after hanging out in the library.

She did have some lingering concerns about going out with one man when she couldn't get a different one out of her mind, but since the day Braden had bought her coffee, she hadn't heard a single word from him. She hadn't seen Ellen or Saige this past week, either, but at least Ellen had called to let her know that they would be absent from Baby Talk and Toddler Time because Saige had a nasty cold and Ellen didn't want her to share it with the other children.

And then, almost as if her thoughts had conjured the woman, Ellen was standing there.

"Who's the lucky guy?" she asked. Then she smiled. "Forgive me for being nosy, but that sounded like you were making plans for a date."

Cassie felt her cheeks flush. "I was. He's the neighbor of a friend."

"Oh," she replied, obviously disappointed. "A blind date?"

Cassie nodded, then asked, "How's Saige doing?"

"Much better," the little girl's grandmother said. "Though it's been a rough week for both of them."

"Both of them?"

"Braden was under the weather, too. Of course, that's what happens when you take care of a sick child. In fact, today will be his first day back at work—he's leaving Saige with me this afternoon and going into the office for a few hours."

"Well, I'm glad to hear they're both doing better—and that you managed to avoid whatever is going around. Because something is definitely going around," she noted. "Even Megan, who never calls in sick, did so today—and we have three school groups coming in for tours and story time this afternoon."

"In that case, I won't keep you from your work any longer," Ellen promised. "I really just wanted to check in to see if Braden stopped by last week to pick up Saige's sock monkey."

"He must have," Cassie told her. "I left it under the desk in a bag with Saige's name on it and it was gone when I got in the next morning."

"So you weren't here when he came in?" the other woman asked, sounding disappointed.

"No, I leave at two on Tuesdays and Thursdays, and then I'm back at seven for Soc & Study," she explained, referring to the teen study group that ran Monday through Friday nights.

Cassie was happy to supervise two nights a week and would have done more if required, because she understood how important it was for students to have a place to escape from the stress and drama of their homes. As a teen with three younger siblings and a short-tempered stepfather, she'd spent as much time as possible at the library. But of course she didn't mention that to Ellen, because she never told anyone about her past, and especially not about Ray.

In an effort to shift the direction of her own thoughts, she said, "Is there anything I can help you find today?"

"I'm just here to pick up a few travel books for Mabel Strauss," Ellen explained. "She hasn't left her own home in more than three years, but she still seems to find joy in planning trips that she's never going to take."

"What's her destination this time?" Cassie asked.

"Japan."

She smiled. "Well, if you're going to dream, dream big, right?"

"Absolutely," Ellen agreed. "Although, in Mabel's case, I think she's just going alphabetically now. It was Italy last week and India the week before that."

"Then you probably don't need me to steer you in the right direction," Cassie noted.

The older woman shook her head. "Thanks, but I know exactly where I'm going."

Several hours later, Cassie wished she wasn't going anywhere. After a busy day, she just wanted to go home, put her feet up and pet her cats. She considered canceling her plans with Darius, but she knew that she'd have to answer to Stacey if she did. She also knew that if she didn't want to spend the rest of her life alone with her cats, she had to get out and meet new people. Specifically, new men.

Unbidden, an image of Braden Garrett formed in her mind. Okay—he was new and she'd met him without leaving the safe haven of the library, but a man who'd lost his first wife in a tragic accident wasn't a good bet for a woman who'd vowed not to be anyone's second choice ever again.

She hadn't dated much since she'd given Joel back his ring. Her former fiancé hadn't just broken her heart, he'd made her question her own judgment. She'd been so wrong about him. Or maybe just so desperate to become a wife and a mother that she'd failed to see the warning signs. She'd fallen for a man who was all wrong for her because she didn't want to be alone.

That realization had taken her aback. For the first ten years of her life, her Army Ranger father had been away more than he'd been home, and her mother—unable to tolerate being alone—had frequently sought out other male companionship. Then her father had been killed overseas and her mother had dated several other men before she'd met and exchanged vows with Ray Houston.

Their marriage had been a volatile one. Naomi was a former beauty queen who basked in the adoration of others; Raymond was proud to show off his beautiful wife and prone to fits of jealousy if she went anywhere without him. Even as a kid, Cassie had decided she'd rather be alone than be anyone's emotional—and sometimes physical— punching bag, and she'd vowed to herself that she wouldn't ever be like her mother, so desperate for a man's attention that she'd put up with his mercurial moods and fiery temper.

For the most part, she was happy on her own and with her life. She had a great job, wonderful friends, and she was content with her own company and the occasional affectionate cuddle with her cats. And then Braden Garrett had walked into the library with his daughter.

So really, it was Braden's fault that she'd agreed to go out with Darius. Because he stirred up all kinds of feelings she'd thought were deeply buried, she'd decided those feelings were a sign that she was ready to start dating again. Because after more than two years on her own, she realized that she wasn't ready to give up. She wanted to fall all the way in love. She wanted to get married and have a family. And while she wasn't all starry-eyed and weak-kneed at the prospect of dinner with Stacey's new neighbor, she wasn't ready to write him off just yet, either.

So she brushed her hair, dabbed some gloss on her lips, spritzed on her perfume and headed out, determined to focus on Darius Richmond and forget about Braden Garrett.

Except that as soon as she walked through the front door of Valentino's, she found herself face-to-face with the man she was trying to forget.

"Hello, Cassie."

She actually halted in mid-stride as the low timbre of his voice made the nerves in her belly quiver. "Mr. Garrett—hi."

He smiled, and her heart started beating double-time. "Braden," he reminded her.

"I…um… What are you doing here?" Her cheeks burned as she stammered out the question. She never stammered, but finding him here—immediately after she'd vowed to put him out of her mind—had her completely flustered.

"Picking up dinner." He held up the take-out bag he carried. "And you?"

"I'm…um…meeting someone." And she was still stammering, she realized, with no small amount of chagrin.

"A date?" Braden guessed.

She nodded, unwilling to trust herself to respond in a complete and coherent sentence.

Of course, that was the precise moment that Darius spotted her. He stood up at the table and waved. She lifted a hand in acknowledgment.

"With Darius Richmond?" The question hinted at both disbelief and disapproval.

"You know him?" And look at that—she'd managed three whole words without a pause or a stutter.

"He went to school with my brother, Ryan," Braden

said, in a tone clearly indicating that he and Stacey's neighbor were *not* friends. "But last I heard, he was living in San Diego."

"He recently moved back to Charisma," she said, repeating what she'd been told.

"How long have you been dating him?"

"I'm not… I mean, this is our first date. And possibly our last, if I keep him waiting much longer." She glanced at the silver bangle watch on her wrist, resisting the urge to squirm beneath Braden's narrow-eyed scrutiny. She had no reason to feel guilty about having dinner with a man. "I was supposed to meet him at seven and it's already ten after."

"He knows you're here," Braden pointed out. "It's not as if he's sitting there, worrying that you've stood him up. Although, if that's what you want to do, I'd be happy to share my penne with sausage and peppers."

"Isn't your daughter waiting for her dinner?" she asked, relieved that she was now managing to uphold her end of the conversation.

But he shook his head. "I worked late trying to catch up after four days away from the office, so she ate with my parents."

"Your mom mentioned that you'd both been under the weather," she noted.

"Saige had the worst of it," he said. "But we're both fully recovered now."

"That's good," she said.

He looked as if he wanted to say something more, but in the end, he only said, "Enjoy your dinner."

"Thanks," Cassie said. "You, too."

Braden forced himself to walk out of the restaurant and drive home, when he really wanted to take his food into the dining room to chaperone Cassie on her date. Unfortunately, he suspected that kind of behavior might edge a little too close to stalking, even if he only wanted to protect her from the womanizing creep.

Because, yeah, he knew Darius Richmond, and he knew the guy had a reputation for using and discarding women. And, yeah, it bothered him that Cassie was on a date with the other man.

Or maybe he was jealous. As uncomfortable as it was to admit, he knew that his feelings were possibly a result of the green-eyed monster rearing its ugly head. Cassie's unwillingness to explore the attraction between them had dented his pride. Discovering that she was on a date with someone else was another unexpected blow, because it proved that she wasn't opposed to dating in general but to dating Braden in particular.

He couldn't figure it out. He knew there was something between them—a definite change in the atmosphere whenever they were in close proximity. What he didn't know was why she was determined to ignore it.

She was great with kids, so he didn't think she was put off by the fact that he had a child. Except that liking children in general was undoubtedly different than dating a guy with a child, and if she had any reservations about that, then she definitely wasn't the right woman for him.

Not that he was looking for "the right woman"—but he wouldn't object to spending time with a woman who was attractive and smart and interested in him. And the only way that was going to happen was if he managed to forget about his attraction to Cassie.

Which meant that he should take a page out of the librarian's book—figuratively speaking—and look for another woman to fulfill his requirement.

The problem was, he didn't want anyone but Cassie.

* * *

Cassie was tidying up the toys in the children's area late Saturday morning when Braden and Saige came into the library. The little girl made a beeline for the train table, where two little boys were already playing. Aside from issuing a firm caution to his daughter to share, Braden seemed content to let her do her own thing. Then he lowered himself onto a plastic stool where he could keep an eye on Saige and near where Cassie was sorting the pieces of several wooden puzzles that had been jumbled together.

"So…how was your date last night?" he asked her.

She continued to sort while she considered her response. "It was an experience," she finally decided.

"That doesn't sound like a rousing endorsement of Darius Richmond."

"Do you really want to hear all of the details?"

"Only if the details are that you had a lousy time and were home by nine o'clock," he told her.

She felt a smile tug at her lips. "Sorry—I wasn't home by nine o'clock." She put three puzzle pieces together. "It was after nine before I left the restaurant and probably closer to nine twenty before I got home."

He smiled. "Nine twenty, huh?"

She nodded.

"Alone?"

She lifted a brow. "I can't believe you just asked me that question."

"A question you haven't answered," he pointed out.

"Yes," she said. "Alone. As I told you last night—it was a first date."

"And you never invite a guy home after a first date?"

"No," she confirmed. "And why don't you like Darius?"

"Because he's a player," Braden said simply.

"So why didn't you tell me that last night?"

"I was tempted to. But if I'd said anything uncompli-
mentary about the man, you might have thought I was trying to sabotage your date, and I was confident that you'd
figure it out quickly enough yourself."

"I knew within the first five minutes that it would be a
first and last date," she admitted.

"What did he do?"

"When I got to the table, he told me that he'd ordered
a glass of wine for me—a California chardonnay that he
assured me I would enjoy. Which maybe I shouldn't fault
him for, because he doesn't know me so how could he
know that I generally prefer red wine over white? And
maybe I wouldn't have minded so much if he was having
a glass of the chardonnay, too, but he was drinking beer."

"You don't like guys who drink beer?" he guessed.

"I don't like guys who assume that women don't drink
beer," she told him.

He nodded. "So noted."

"And when the waitress came to tell us about the daily
specials, his gaze kept slipping from her face to her chest."

"You should have walked out then," he told her.

"Probably," she agreed. "Then he ordered calamari as
an appetizer for us to share. And I hate squid."

"But again, he didn't ask you," Braden guessed, glancing over at the train table to check on his daughter.

"Not only did he not ask—he ignored my protests, as
if he knew what I wanted more than I did.

"But still, I was hopeful that the evening could be sal-
vaged," she admitted. "Because Valentino's does the most
amazing three-cheese tortellini in a tomato cream sauce.
And when I gave my order to the waitress—vetoing his
suggestion of the veal Marsala—he suggested, with a bla-
tantly lewd wink, that I would have to follow my meal

with some intense physical activity to burn off all of the calories in the entrée."

Braden's gaze narrowed. "Is *that* when you walked out?"

"No," she denied. "I ordered the tortellini—with garlic bread—and I ate every single bite."

He chuckled. "Good for you."

"Then I had cheesecake for dessert, put money on the table for my meal and said good-night. And he seemed genuinely baffled to discover that I didn't intend to go home with him." She shook her head. "I mean, it was obvious early on that the date was a disaster, and yet he still thought I'd sleep with him?"

"When it comes to sex, men are eternally optimistic creatures."

"He was more delusional than optimistic if he believed for even two seconds that I would get naked with him after he counted the calories of every bite I put in my mouth."

"Note to self—never comment on a woman's food choices."

"I'm sure you didn't need to be told that."

"You're right," he admitted. "But obviously I'm doing something wrong, because you shot me down when I asked you to go out with me."

"You never actually asked me out," she said.

He frowned at that. "I'm sure I did."

She shook her head. "You only asked what we should do about the chemistry between us."

"And you said the chemistry would fizzle," he said, apparently remembering that part of the conversation.

She nodded.

"But it hasn't," he noted.

She kept her focus on the puzzles she was assembling.

"So what do you propose we do now?"

"Right now, I'm trying to figure out how to tell Stacey that last night's date was a complete bust," she admitted.

"You could tell her you met someone that you like more," he suggested.

She finally looked up to find his gaze on her. "I do like you," she admitted. "But you're a widower with a child."

He frowned. "Which part of that equation is a problem for you?"

"It doesn't really matter which part, does it?" she said, sincerely regretful.

"You're right," he agreed. "But I'd still like to know."

Thankfully, before he could question her further, Saige came running over with a train clenched in each fist.

"Choo-choo," she said, in a demand for her daddy to play with her.

And Cassie took advantage of the opportunity to escape.

Chapter Six

She wasn't proud of the way she'd ended her conversation with Braden, but she'd done what she needed to do. If she tried to explain her reasons and her feelings, he might try to change her mind. And there was a part of her—the huge empty space in her heart—that wished he would.

She left the library early that afternoon and headed over to Serenity Gardens. When she arrived at the residence, she saw that a group of women of various shapes and sizes was participating in some kind of dance class in the front courtyard. Some were in sweats and others in spandex, and while they didn't seem to be particularly well choreographed, they all looked like they were having a good time.

"Geriatric Jazzercise," a familiar male voice said from behind her.

Cassie choked on a laugh as she turned to Jerry. "That's not really what they call it?"

He held up a hand as if taking an oath. "It really is."

"Well, exercise is important at any age," she acknowledged. "Unfortunately, I can't imagine Irene participating in something like this."

"Can't you?" he asked, his eyes twinkling. "Check out the woman in the striped purple top."

Cassie looked more closely at the group, her eyes widening when they zeroed in on and finally recognized the former librarian. "I don't know what to say," she admitted.

"You could say you'll have a cup of coffee with me," Jerry told her. "As I was told, in clear and unequivocal terms, that the jazzercise class is for women only."

"I'd be happy to have coffee with you," Cassie said, falling into step beside Jerry as he headed back toward the building.

"What's that you've got there?" he asked, indicating the hardback in her hand. "A new book for Irene?"

She nodded. "One of the advantages of being head librarian—I get dibs on the new releases when they come in."

"My name's on the waiting list for that one," he admitted.

"Irene's a fast reader—maybe she'll let you borrow it when she's done."

"I'm a fast reader, too," he told her. "Maybe *I* could give it to Irene when *I'm* done."

"That would work," she agreed.

Peggy's Bakery and Coffee Shop, on the ground floor of the residence, offered a variety of hot and cold beverages and baked goods, and the air was permeated with the mouthwatering scents of coffee and chocolate.

"What will you have?" Jerry asked her.

Cassie perused the menu, pleased to note that they had her favorite. "A vanilla latte, please."

"And I'll have a regular decaf," Jerry said.

"Can I interest you in a couple of triple chocolate brownies still warm from the oven?" Peggy asked.

"One for sure," Jerry immediately responded, before glancing at Cassie in a silent question.

"Brownies are my weakness," she admitted.

"Make it two," he said.

"You go ahead and grab a seat," Peggy said. "I'll bring everything out to you."

"Can we sit outside?" Cassie asked.

"Anywhere you like," the other woman assured them.

They sat on opposite sides of a small round table, beneath a green-and-white-striped awning. Peggy delivered their coffee and brownies only a few minutes later.

Jerry poured two packets of sugar into his coffee, stirred. "The first time I saw you here, visiting Irene, I thought you must be her granddaughter. Then I found out that she never married, never had any children."

"No, she didn't," Cassie confirmed.

"So what is your relationship?" he wondered. "If you don't mind me asking."

"I don't mind," she told him. "And although our relationship has changed a lot over the years, Irene has always played an important part in my life—from librarian to confidante, surrogate mother, mentor and friend."

"You've known her a long time then?"

"Since I was in fourth grade."

"I've known her a long time, too," Jerry said. "We grew up across the street from one another in the west end, went to school together, dated for a while when we were in high school. I'm sure both my parents and hers thought we would marry someday." He cut off a piece of brownie with his fork. "In fact, I was planning to propose to her at Christmas, the year after we graduated."

"What happened?"

He chewed on the brownie for a long minute, his eyes focused on something—or maybe some time—in the distance. "I met someone else that summer and fell head over heels in love." He shifted his attention back to Cassie, his gaze almost apologetic. "I'd fallen in love with Irene slowly, over a lot of years. And then Faith walked into my life and the emotions hit me like a ton of bricks. Everything with her was new and intense and exciting."

"And you married her instead," Cassie guessed.

He nodded. "She was the love of my life and I'm grateful for the almost fifty years we had together."

"And now you've come full circle," she noted.

"Do you disapprove of my friendship with Irene?"

"Of course not," she denied. "But I don't want to see her get hurt again."

"Neither do I," he told her.

She considered his response as she nibbled on her own brownie, savoring the rich chocolate flavor.

"Have you ever been in love, Cassie?"

"I was engaged once."

"Which isn't necessarily the same thing," he pointed out.

"I haven't had much luck in the love department," she acknowledged.

"It only takes once," he told her. "You only need one forever-after love to change your whole life."

She sipped her coffee. "I'll keep that in mind."

"It's not about the mind," Jerry admonished. "It's about the heart. You have to keep an open heart."

Cassie thought about Jerry's advice for a long time after she'd said goodbye to him and left Serenity Gardens. A week later, his words continued to echo in the back of her mind.

She headed to the library much earlier than usual, eager to get started on the setup for the Book & Bake Sale. The forecast was for partly sunny skies with a 25 percent chance of precipitation, but that was not until late afternoon. Cassie hoped they would be sold out and packed up before then.

The event was scheduled to start at 8:00 a.m. but she was on-site by six thirty to meet with a group of volunteers from the high school to set up the tents and the tables. There were boxes and boxes in the library basement—old books that had been taken out of circulation and donations from the community.

Over the past several weeks, Tanya and a couple of her friends from the high school had sorted through the donations, grouping the books into genres. Some of the books were horribly outdated—such as *Understanding Windows 2000*—but she decided to put them out on display anyway, because local crafters often picked up old books to create new things. In addition to the books, there were board games and toys and DVDs.

The student volunteers were almost finished setting up the tents when Braden showed up just after seven. It was the first time she'd seen him since she'd abruptly ended their conversation the previous Saturday morning—though she'd heard from Megan that he'd checked out some books when she was on her lunch break a few days earlier—and she wasn't sure what to make of his presence here now.

"The sale doesn't start until eight," she told him.

"I know, but I thought you might be able to use an extra hand with set up."

"We can always use extra hands," she admitted.

"So put me to work," he suggested.

"Where's Saige?" she asked.

"Having pancakes at my parents' house."

"Lucky girl."

He smiled. "My mom's going to bring her by later."

"Okay," she said. "Most of the tents have been set up, Tanya and Chloe know how to arrange the tables, which Cade and Jake are bringing out, so why don't you help Ethan and Tyler haul boxes up from the basement?"

"I can do that," he confirmed.

She led him down to the basement and introduced him to the other helpers, then went back outside to help Brooke arrange the goodies on the bake table. With so many volunteers from the high school—most of them students who were regulars at Soc & Study—there wasn't a lot for her to do, and she found herself spending an inordinate amount of time watching Braden and pretending that she wasn't.

"Is there somewhere else you're supposed to be?" he asked, when he caught her glancing at her watch for about the tenth time.

"Serenity Gardens in half an hour."

"Aren't you about fifty years too early for Serenity Gardens?"

"So maybe we were talking about the same Miss Houlahan," he mused.

"She's been retired for several years, but she never misses any of our fund-raising events."

"I didn't know she was still alive," he admitted. "She seemed about a hundred years old when I was a kid."

"I'm seventy-one," a sharp voice said from behind him. "And not ready for the grave yet."

Braden visibly winced before turning around. "Miss Houlahan—how lovely to see you again."

Behind square wire-rimmed glasses, the old woman's pale blue eyes narrowed. "You're just as cheeky now as you were when you were a boy, Braden Garrett."

Cassie seemed as surprised as he was that the former librarian had remembered him well enough to be able to distinguish him from his brothers and male cousins—all of whom bore a striking resemblance to one another.

"I was planning to pick you up," Cassie interjected.

"Jerry decided he wanted to come and get some books, and it didn't make sense to drag you away if he was heading in this direction," Miss Houlahan said.

"Where is Mr. Riordan?"

"He dropped me off in front, then went to park the car."

"Well, we're not quite finished setting up, but you're welcome to wander around and browse through the books we've got on display."

"I'm not here to shop, I'm here to work," Irene said abruptly.

Cassie nodded, unfazed by the woman's brusque demeanor. "Was there any particular section you wanted to work in?" she asked solicitously.

"Put me near history," the former librarian suggested. "Most people assume old people are experts on anything old."

"We've got history set up—" Cassie glanced at the tables queued along the sideway "—four tables over, just this side of the card shop. Give me a second to finish this display and I'll show you."

"I've got a box of history books right here," Braden said. "I can show her."

"It's 'Miss Houlahan' not 'her,'" Irene corrected him. "And I know where the card shop is."

"I'm heading in that direction anyway, *Miss Houlahan*," he told her.

But she'd already turned and started to walk away, her steps slow and methodical, her right hand gripping the handle of a nondescript black cane. Braden fell into step beside her, the box propped on his shoulder so that he had a hand free in case *Miss Houlahan* stumbled.

She didn't say two words to him as they made their way down the sidewalk. Not that they were going very far—the history/political science table wasn't more than thirty feet from the library's main doors—and not that he expected her to entertain him with chatter, but the silence was somehow not just uncomfortable but somehow disapproving. Or maybe he was projecting his childhood memories onto the moment.

When they reached the table, he eased the box from his shoulder and dropped it on the ground, perhaps a little more loudly than was necessary, and got a perverse sense of pleasure when she jolted at the noise, then glared at him. As he busied himself unpacking the books, he reminded himself that he was no longer a child easily intimidated but a CEO more accustomed to intimidating other people.

He'd just finished unpacking when he heard the sweetest sound in the world: "Da-da!"

Tucking the now-empty box under the table, he turned just in time to catch Saige as she launched herself into his arms. "There's my favorite girl," he said, giving her a light squeeze.

"Choo-choo, Da-da! Choo-choo!" she implored.

"Later," he promised.

Unhappy with his response, she turned her attention to her grandmother, who was following closely behind her. "Choo-choo, Ga-ma!"

"We can go find the trains in a minute," Ellen told her, before greeting Irene Houlahan.

While his mother was chatting with the old librarian, Braden slipped away to get a chair for Miss Houlahan. By the time he got back, his mother and Saige were gone again.

Miss Houlahan thanked him, somewhat stiffly, for the chair before she said, "Your daughter doesn't look much like you."

He smiled at her blunt statement of the obvious fact that so many other people tried to tiptoe around. "Her paternal grandmother was Japanese."

"You adopted her then?" she guessed.

He nodded.

"Adoption is a wonderful way to match up parents who want a child with a child who needs a family," she noted.

He appreciated not just the sentiment but her word choice. He didn't want to count the number of times that someone had referred to children placed for adoption as "unwanted," because that description couldn't be further from the truth. Perhaps untimely in the lives of the women who birthed them, those babies were desperately wanted by their adoptive parents. And in the case of his own daughter, he knew that Lindsay had wanted her child but, even more, she'd wanted a better life for Saige than she'd felt she would be able to give her.

"There was a time I considered adopting a child myself," Miss Houlahan surprised him by confiding. "But that was about forty years ago, when unmarried women weren't considered suitable to take on the responsibilities of raising a child, except maybe a child who was in the foster care system."

"I'm not sure much has changed," he admitted.

"Back then, not a lot of men would be willing to raise an infant on their own, either," she noted.

"I'm a Garrett," he reminded her. "There are currently thirty-one members of my immediate family in this town—believe me, I haven't done any of this on my own."

Miss Houlahan smiled at that, the upward curve of her lips immediately softening her usually stern and disapproving expression. "It takes a village," she acknowledged. "And a willingness to rely on that village."

"Believe me, I'm not just willing but grateful. I don't know how I would have managed otherwise."

"Where does Cassie fit into the picture?" Irene asked.

He didn't insult her by pretending to misunderstand the question. "I'd say that's up to her."

"Hmm," she said. Before she could expand on that response, a tall, silver-haired man ambled over. "I let you out of my sight for five minutes, and you're already chatting up other men," he teased Miss Houlahan.

She pursed her lips in obvious disapproval but introduced the newcomer as Jerry Riordan to Braden, and the two men shook hands.

"You're not trying to steal away my girl, are you?" Jerry asked.

Braden held up his hands in surrender. "No, sir. I can promise you that."

"I'm not anyone's *girl* and I'm not *your* anything," Miss Houlahan said firmly to her contemporary. "And Braden has his eye on Cassie."

"Then I'd say he's got a good eye," Jerry said, sending a conspiratorial wink in Braden's direction.

Miss Houlahan sniffed disapprovingly. "She's a lot more than a pretty face, and she deserves a man who appreciates her sharp mind and generous heart, too."

Braden silently acknowledged the validity of her concerns, because as much as he appreciated Cassie's pretty face and sharp mind, he had no interest in her heart—and even less in putting his own on the line again.

Chapter Seven

The library didn't spend much money to advertise the Book & Bake Sale, relying mostly on word of mouth to draw people to the event. As Cassie looked around the crowds gathered at the tables and milling on the sidewalk, she was satisfied the strategy had succeeded.

She wandered over to the children's tent—always one of the more popular sections—where, in addition to the books and games and toys for sale, balloon animals were being made and happy faces were being painted. Chloe, a straight-A student and an incredible artist, was turning boys and girls into various jungle animals and superheroes, and the lineup for this transformation seemed endless. While Cassie was there, a pint-size dark-haired toddler came racing toward her, baring tiny white teeth. "Raar!"

In response to the growl, Cassie hunkered down to the child's level. "Well, who is this?" she asked, peering closely at the little girl's face. "She looks a little bit like Saige and a lot like a scary lion."

"Raar!" Saige said again, then held out the train in her hand for Cassie's perusal.

"What have you got there?"

"Choo-choo."

She glanced at Braden. "Daddy finally caved and bought you a train, did he?"

Though the little girl probably didn't understand all of the words, she nodded enthusiastically.

"Not Daddy, Grandma," he corrected. "My mother spoils her rotten."

"If that was true, she'd be rotten and she's not," Ellen Garrett protested as she joined them. "In fact, she's so sweet I could gobble her right up." Then she scooped up her granddaughter and pretended to nibble on her shoulder, making Saige shriek with laughter.

"That doesn't change the fact that you indulge her every whim," Braden pointed out.

"Unfortunately, I can't give her what she really needs," his mother said.

He sighed. "Mom."

The single word was a combination of wariness and warning that gave Cassie the distinct impression she was in the middle of a familiar argument between the son and his mother.

"But I can give her a cookie," Ellen said, apparently heeding the warning.

"Kee?" Saige echoed hopefully.

Braden nodded. "*One* cookie," he agreed. "And then I need to get her home for her nap."

"I can take her back to my house," Ellen offered.

"You already had her for most of the morning," he pointed out.

"Is there a reason I shouldn't spend more time with my granddaughter?"

"You know there isn't," he said. "And you know how much I appreciate everything you do for us."

Cassie kept her attention on Saige, quietly entertaining the little girl with the "Handful of Fingers" song while her father and grandmother sorted out their plans.

"Then maybe you could do something for me," his mother suggested.

"Of course," he agreed readily.

"Stick around here to help Cassie with the cleanup—and make sure she gets something to eat."

"Oh, that isn't necessary," Cassie interjected. "We have plenty of volunteers."

"But you can always use extra hands," Braden reminded her of the statement she'd made only a few hours earlier.

"That's settled then," Ellen said happily. "Come on, Saige. Let's go get that cookie."

Braden stole a hug and a kiss from his daughter before he let her head off to the bake table with her grandmother.

"You really don't have to stay," Cassie told him. "You've already done so much to help."

"I do need to stay—my mother said so."

She smiled at that. "Do you always do what your mother tells you to?"

"Usually," he acknowledged. "Especially when it's what I want to do, anyway."

"There must be something else you'd rather do with your Saturday."

"You don't think supporting a community fund-raiser for the local library is good use of my time?" he countered.

"You're deliberately misunderstanding me."

"And you're tiptoeing around the question you really want to ask," he told her.

"You're right," she agreed, a teasing glint in her eye. "What I really want to know is why you got arrested."

He frowned. "Why would you think I was arrested?"

"Because your sudden determination to volunteer seems like a community service thing to me," she told him.

He chuckled at that. "You really do have a suspicious mind, don't you?"

"Not suspicious so much as skeptical," she told him.

"I wanted to help out," he said. "Although yes, I did have an ulterior motive."

"I knew it."

"To spend some time with you," he said, and slung a companionable arm across her shoulders. "Now let's go see if there's anything left at the bake table."

"There's probably not much more than crumbs," she warned. "I know for a fact that all of Mrs. Bowman's muffins were gone within the first half hour."

"How many of those did you take?"

"Four."

He lifted his brows. "Two were my breakfast," she explained. "I took the other two for Irene and Jerry."

"And none for me," he lamented.

"Sorry."

"You can make it up to me by going out with me for some real food when this is over and done," he suggested.

"Are you asking me on a date?"

"I am," he confirmed.

"Then I'm sorry to have to decline," she said. "Because the only reason half these kids are here to help with the takedown is that they know I always get pizza and soda for the volunteers when we're done."

"Does that mean I get to hang around for pizza and soda?"

"Only if you stop slacking and get back to work," she told him.

He grinned. "Yes, ma'am."

* * *

Cassie couldn't fault his work ethic. Braden did what he was told and with a lot less grumbling than she got from some of the teens who were helping out. He might spend his days sitting behind a desk, but he didn't look soft. In fact, the way his muscles bunched and flexed while he worked, he looked pretty darn mouthwatering and close to perfect.

And if she felt uncomfortable that he was hanging around, well, that was on her. He'd done absolutely nothing to suggest that his reasons for being there weren't as simple and straightforward as he claimed. But every once in a while, she'd catch a glimpse of him out of the corner of her eye, and she'd feel a little tingle course through her veins. Or she'd find him looking at her and he'd smile, unashamed to be caught staring, and her heart would flutter inside her chest as if she was a teenage girl. And maybe being surrounded by so many fifteen-to-seventeen year-olds was the reason for her immature and emotional response to the man.

"Is everything okay, Miss Mac?"

She dragged her attention away from Braden to focus on Ethan Anderson—a senior honor student and first-string football player. "Of course, Ethan."

"Who's the old guy hanging around?"

She couldn't help but smile at that. Not because Braden was old but because she understood that to most teens anyone over thirty was ancient—a status she was close to attaining herself. "Braden Garrett," she said. "His daughter is in a couple of the preschool programs."

"Is he your boyfriend?"

"No," she said quickly, unexpectedly flustered by the question.

"Then why is he here?" Ethan wanted to know.

"To help out," she said. "Just like everyone else."

"He's keeping a closer eye on you than anyone else," the teen noted.

"The tables," she reminded him, attempting to shift his attention back to the task at hand.

"You told me to keep this one set up for the pizza."

"Oh. Right."

Ethan eyed her speculatively, his lips curving. "Maybe he's not your boyfriend, but you like him, don't you?"

"What?" She pretended not to understand what he was asking, but she suspected the flush in her cheeks proved otherwise.

"I just noticed that you're keeping a pretty close eye on him, too," he remarked.

"It's my responsibility to keep an eye on *all* of the volunteers," she reminded him.

"So why haven't you told Cade and Jake to stop fooling around?"

She hadn't even noticed that the fifteen-year-old twins were roughhousing on the other side of the room until Ethan directed her gaze in that direction. "Cade, Jake," she called out. "If you don't stop fooling around, I won't sign off on your volunteer hours."

Cade reluctantly released his brother from his headlock and Jake took his elbow out of his twin's side.

Ethan's smile only widened.

Thankfully, before he could say anything else, Tanya announced that the pizza had arrived. While she and Chloe got out the drinks and plates and napkins, Cassie took out the money she'd tucked into her pocket. But when she looked up again, the delivery guy was already halfway back to his car.

"I didn't pay him," Cassie said, frowning.

"I did," Braden told her.

"You didn't have to do that—I've got the money right here."

But he shook his head when she tried to give it to him. "I'm beginning to suspect this might be the only way I ever get to buy you dinner."

Before she could respond, the volunteers descended on the boxes.

"You better grab a slice while you can," she told him.

He nodded and reached for a plate.

Although Braden knew this wasn't quite what his mother had in mind when she asked him to make sure that Cassie got something to eat, he was glad he'd stayed. Not only to lend a hand but to see her interact with the teen group. Although she was an authority figure, he could tell that they didn't just respect her, they genuinely liked her. And they were undoubtedly curious about who he was and why he was hanging around.

There was a lot of talk and laughter while everyone chowed down. The kids were an eclectic group: there was the good girl, the jock, the geek, the cheerleader, the artist. They probably didn't interact much at school, if their paths crossed at all, but here they were all—if not friends—at least friendly.

"Who's the kid in the red hoodie with the fat lip and angry glare?" he asked.

"That's Kevin," Cassie told him. "An eleventh grader at Southmount."

"What's his story?"

She looked at him curiously. "Why do you think he has any more of a story than any of the other kids here?"

"The way you look at him—like you understand what he's all about," he said.

"He hangs out at the library because he's got four

younger siblings at home, it's not all that difficult to understand," she told him.

Maybe not, but he suspected it wasn't quite that simple, either. "What happened to his lip?"

She shrugged. "How would I know?"

But her deliberately casual tone made him suspect that she did know—and wasn't nearly as unconcerned as she wanted him to believe.

"Does he get knocked around at home?" he asked quietly.

"Again—how would I know?"

But he saw it, just a flicker in her eyes, before she answered. And he realized that not only did she know, she'd been there. Who? When? These questions and more clamored for answers, but he knew this wasn't the time and place. Instead, he reached for another slice of pizza.

When everyone had eaten their fill, Cassie wrapped up the extra slices and discreetly slipped them into certain backpacks. After the food was cleared away, the teens started to head out.

Braden noticed that Ethan was the last to leave—after carrying the sole remaining table to the library basement, and even then he seemed reluctant to go.

"Are you sure you don't need anything else, Miss Mac?" the teen asked Cassie.

"I'm sure," she said. "Thanks for all of your help today."

"Anytime," Ethan said.

"So long as it's before June, right?" Cassie said. "After you graduate, you'll be throwing a football at college somewhere."

"Ohio State University," he told her proudly. "I'm going to be a Buckeye."

"Congratulations, Ethan. That's wonderful news."

"I'm glad you think so—Alyssa isn't so thrilled."

"Because she's got another year of high school before she goes off to college," Cassie acknowledged. "But I know she's proud of you."

Ethan checked his phone, grimaced. "And she's going to be annoyed with me if I'm late picking her up for our date tonight."

"Then you should get going," she advised.

He nodded, casting a sidelong glance toward Braden before he headed out. "Have a good night, Miss Mac."

"I don't think your football player likes me," Braden noted.

"He doesn't know you," Cassie clarified, heading into the building.

He followed. "And he's very protective of you."

"He does have a protective nature," she agreed. "But he's a good kid." She sighed when she saw the empty boxes all over the basement but didn't say anything else as she picked one up and broke it apart.

Braden picked up another and did the same. "I noticed most of the kids call you Miss Mac."

"They like nicknames."

But he knew it was more than that—it was a sign of acceptance and camaraderie. "I wonder if anyone ever considered giving Miss Houlahan a nickname," he mused. "How does 'Hoolie' sound?"

"Not very flattering," she said, but he could tell she was fighting a smile.

He grinned. "You don't think she'd like it?"

"I think you like to rile Miss Houlahan," she said, continuing to collapse the empty boxes.

"She was all about the rules and I was never a big fan of them," he explained.

"Your tune will change in a few years," Cassie warned

him. "When your daughter grows up and boys start coming around."

"Nah, I'll just put a padlock on her bedroom door," he decided.

"And then she'll sneak out her bedroom window," she warned.

"Is that what you did when you wanted to go out with a guy you knew your father wouldn't approve of?"

She shook her head. "My dad died when I was ten."

"I'm sorry."

"It was a long time ago," she said.

"Still, I imagine that losing a parent isn't an experience you forget about after a few years."

"No," she agreed. "But you shouldn't worry that Saige will be scarred by the loss of her mother—she's obviously happy and well loved."

"I wasn't thinking about Saige but about you," he told her.

"It was a long time ago," she said again.

She'd left only the biggest box intact and now stuffed the folded cardboard inside of it. "Thanks for your help today. We usually have a good number of volunteers, but the kids sometimes forget why they're here, so it was nice to have another adult around to keep them on task."

"You have an interesting group of kids," he said, turning his attention to stacking the stray chairs with the others that lined the wall. "I couldn't help but notice that they come from several different area high schools."

She nodded. "We advertise our programs widely—in all the schools and at local rec centers—to ensure all students are aware of our programs. For the most part, the ones who come here want the same thing, so they don't bring their issues or rivalries inside."

"That's impressive," he said. "Kids usually carry their grudges wherever they go."

"Only kids?" she challenged, doing a final visual scan of the basement.

"No." He breached the short distance that separated them. "But most adults have better impulse control."

She tipped her head back to meet his gaze. "You think so?"

"Usually," he clarified.

And then he gave in to his own impulses and kissed her.

Cassie was caught completely unaware.

One minute they were having a friendly conversation while they tidied up the basement storage area, and the next, his mouth had swooped down on hers.

In that first moment of contact, her heart stuttered and her mind went blank. And somehow, without even knowing what she was doing, she wound her arms around his neck and kissed him back.

It was all the encouragement Braden needed. He slid his hands around her back, drawing her closer. Close enough that her breasts grazed his chest, making her nipples tighten and the nerves in her belly quiver.

She was suddenly, achingly aware that it had been more than two years since she'd had sex. Twenty-eight months since she'd experienced the thrill of tangling the sheets with a man. For most of that time, she hadn't missed the sharing of physical intimacy. Truth be told, she'd barely thought about it.

But she was definitely thinking about it now.

Braden tipped her head back and adjusted the angle of his mouth on hers, taking his time to deepen the kiss and explore her flavor. Her fingers tangled in the silky ends of his hair, holding on to him as the world tilted on its axis. She sighed and his tongue delved between her parted lips to dance with hers in an erotically enticing rhythm.

He was turning her inside out with a single kiss, obliterating her ability to think. And she needed to think. She needed to be smart. And inviting this man to her home, to her bed, would not be smart.

But it would feel good.

If the man made love even half as masterfully as he kissed, she had no doubt that it would feel *really* good.

She forced herself to push that taunting, tempting thought aside, and to finally, reluctantly, push him away, too.

"What…" She took a moment to catch her breath. "What was that?"

"I think that's what happens when you try to douse a flame with gasoline," he said, sounding a little breathless himself.

"Explosive."

He nodded. "And proof that the chemistry between us hasn't fizzled. You're a dangerous woman, Cassie Mac-Kinnon."

"Me? You're the one who started the fire."

"You're the first woman I've kissed in fifteen months," he admitted. "You're the only woman—aside from my wife—that I've kissed in eight years."

The ground was starting to feel a little more stable beneath her feet, but her heart was still struggling to find a normal rhythm. "That might explain why your technique is a little rusty."

But her unsteady tone belied her words, and his smile widened. "I'd be happy to show you a few other unpracticed talents."

She put her hand on his chest, holding him at a distance. "Maybe another time."

"Is that an invitation or a brush-off?" he asked.

She blew out a breath. "I'm not sure."

Chapter Eight

Several hours later, Braden couldn't stop thinking about the scorching hot kiss he'd shared with the sexy librarian.

Finally back home after picking Saige up from his parents' house and settling her into her crib, he sat down in front of the television as he did on so many other nights. Impulsively, he picked up the remote, clicked off the power and picked up the book he'd borrowed from the library.

But half an hour later, he hadn't turned a single page. He couldn't focus on the words because he couldn't stop thinking about Cassie. He closed the cover and set it aside.

Maybe he shouldn't have kissed her.

Maybe he shouldn't have *stopped* kissing her.

Maybe he should have his head examined.

Definitely he should have his head examined.

He wasn't accustomed to indecision. He was a Garrett—and Garretts didn't vacillate. Garretts set goals and devised clear strategies to get what they wanted.

Braden wanted Cassie, and he didn't doubt that she wanted him, too. But while he was confident that taking her to bed would satisfy their most immediate and basic needs, he knew that he had to think about what would happen after.

He wanted sex. After sleeping alone for more than fifteen months, he desperately wanted the blissful pleasure of joining together with a warm, willing woman. But he wanted more than that, too. One of the things he missed most about being married was the companionship—having someone to talk with about his day, someone to eat dinner with and watch TV with. Someone to snuggle with at night—not necessarily as a prelude to sex but as an affirmation that he wasn't alone in the world.

Oh, who was he kidding? A man snuggled when he wanted sex—other than that, he didn't want anyone encroaching on his territory. Except that after sleeping alone in his king-size bed for so many months, he realized he might not object to a little encroaching. Especially if Cassie was the one invading his space.

If he closed his eyes, he could picture her there—in his bedroom, sprawled on top of the covers in the middle of his mattress, wearing nothing but a smile. He didn't dare close his eyes.

The fact that she was acquainted with his mother and his daughter was both a comfort and a complication. If he decided to pursue a relationship with the librarian, he knew he wouldn't face any obstacles from his family. But if he subsequently screwed up that relationship, it could be incredibly awkward for all of them.

He wasn't looking for a one-night stand, but he wasn't looking to fall in love, either. He had no desire to go down that path again. And while he wasn't opposed to the idea of sharing his life with someone special, his main focus right now was Saige and what was best for his little girl.

But when he finally did sleep, it was Cassie who played the starring role in his dreams.

After she'd finished catching Irene up on all the latest happenings at the library and read a couple chapters of a new book to her, Cassie headed to the grocery store to do her weekly shopping. With her list in hand, she methodically walked up and down the aisles.

She paused at the meat cooler and surveyed the selection of pork roasts. Several weeks earlier, she'd found a recipe that she was eager to try, but the roasts seemed like too much for one person. Of course, she could freeze the leftovers for future meals—or maybe invite Irene and Jerry to come over.

After selecting what she needed from that department, she moved to the fresh food section and from there on to the nonperishable aisles. Cat food was on sale, so she stocked up on Westley's and Buttercup's favorite flavors. Then she remembered that she needed kitty litter, too, and added a bag of that to her cart.

And then she rounded the corner and nearly collided with Braden Garrett.

"I guess it's a popular day for grocery shopping," she said lightly.

Saige was seated in the cart facing her father, but twisted around when she recognized Cassie's voice, a wide smile spreading across her face.

"I'm here at least three times a week," Braden admitted. "Because I never seem to remember everything I need to get it all done in one trip."

"You don't make a list?"

"I usually do, and then I usually forget the list on the table at home."

Cassie smiled as Saige offered her a package of string cheese. "Those look yummy," she commented.

The little girl nodded her enthusiastic agreement.

"What other treats does Daddy have for you in there?"

Saige dropped the package of cheese and picked up a box of yogurt tubes. "Chay-wee."

The flavor noted on the box helped Cassie interpret. "You like the cherry ones best," she guessed.

Saige nodded again.

"Me, too," Cassie confided, as she glanced from Braden's shopping cart to her own. His was almost filled with family-size boxes of cereal, multipacks of juice, and bags of fresh fruits and vegetables; Cassie's basket wasn't even half full and her biggest purchases were the cat food and kitty litter.

"We're on our way to the prepared foods section, because I forgot to take dinner out of the freezer this morning," Braden told her. "Why don't you come over to eat with us?"

"Thanks, but I have to get my groceries home and put away."

"You could come over after," he suggested.

She considered the offer for about two seconds before declining. Because as much as she didn't want to be the lonely old cat lady, she also didn't want to be the broken-hearted librarian. Again. And since the kiss they'd shared in the basement of the library four days earlier, it would be foolish to continue to deny the chemistry between them. The only thing she could do now was avoid situations in which that chemistry might heat up again.

"I could get a tray of three-cheese tortellini," he said enticingly. "It's not Valentino's, but it's not bad."

She ignored the temptation—of the food and the man. "Maybe another time."

His direct and steady gaze warned that he could read more of what she was thinking and feeling than she wanted him to.

"We're at twenty-eight Spruceside in Forrest Hill, if you change your mind," he finally said.

But she knew that she wouldn't—she couldn't. "Enjoy your tortellini."

When Cassie was finished making and eating her own dinner, she turned on her tablet to check her email. Then she snapped a picture of the cats wrestling on the carpet in front of her and posted it to her Facebook page. Scrolling through her newsfeed, she saw that a friend from high school—who had married in the Bahamas just before Christmas—was expecting a baby. She noted her congratulations, adding hearts and celebratory confetti emojis to the message.

Buttercup jumped up onto the couch and crawled into her lap. She stroked her back, her feline companion purring contentedly as Cassie's fingers slid through her soft, warm fur.

She had so many reasons to be grateful: terrific friends and a great job that allowed her to spend much of her time working with children. But recently, after spending even just a little bit of time with Braden and Saige, she was suddenly aware of the emptiness inside herself, a yearning for something more.

She was twenty-nine years old with a history of broken or dead-end relationships—it would be crazy to even think about getting involved with a widowed single father to an adorable baby girl who made all of her maternal instincts sit up and beg "pick me." And while Braden had flirted with her a little, and kissed her exactly once, she didn't know what he wanted from her. But she knew what she wanted: a husband, children, a house with a second chair on the front porch and a tire swing in the backyard.

Unfortunately, she had a habit of jumping into relationships, falling in love before she had a chance to catch her breath. Most of the time, it was infatuation rather than love, but she usually only realized the truth after the relationship was over.

She wondered whether it was some kind of legacy from her childhood, if losing her family had created a desperate yearning in her for a meaningful connection. She didn't have a list of qualities that she was looking for in a partner, although she wouldn't object to meeting a man who would make her heart beat from across a room and her insides quiver with a simple touch—and Braden Garrett checked both of those boxes.

She also liked the way he interacted with his little girl, leaving absolutely no doubt about how much he loved his daughter. And she liked the way he talked about his family—not just his parents and siblings but his aunts, uncles and cousins and all of their kids.

And she really liked the way she felt when he looked at her.

She hadn't felt that stir of attraction in a long time—and she didn't want to be feeling it for this man now. Because as gorgeous and charming as he was, she'd vowed to stay away from men who had already given their hearts away.

But she couldn't deny that she was intrigued to see his house in Forrest Hill—or maybe she was just looking for an excuse to see him again. Whatever the reason, she set her tablet aside and picked up her keys.

Braden settled Saige into her high chair with a bowl of tortellini while he put the groceries away. She used both of her hands to shove the stuffed pasta into her mouth, ignoring the spoon he'd given to her. When her bowl was empty, she had sauce—and a happy grin—spread across her face.

"Did you like that?" he asked her.

She nodded and pushed her empty bowl to the edge of her tray. "Mo'."

"Do you want more pasta or do you want dessert?"

She didn't hesitate. "Zert!"

"Yeah, that was a tough question, wasn't it?" He chuckled as he wiped her face, hands and tray.

He was looking in the fridge, considering dessert options, when the doorbell rang.

He unbuckled Saige and lifted her out of her high chair, then went to respond to the summons. He wasn't expecting company, but it wasn't unusual for his parents or his brother Justin, or any of his cousins to stop by if they were in the neighborhood. The absolute last person he expected to see when he opened the door was Charisma's sexy librarian.

"I changed my mind," Cassie said.

Despite the assertion, she looked a little uncertain, as if she might again change her mind and turn right back around.

"I'm glad," he said, and moved away from the door so that she could enter. "Saige and I have already eaten, but there is some pasta left."

"Zert!" Saige said.

Cassie smiled at his daughter. "I had dinner," she said. "And then I decided I was in the mood for ice cream, so I went back to the grocery store and came out with all of this."

He glanced at the bags as she stepped into the foyer. "That looks like a lot of ice cream."

"It's not just ice cream. There's also chocolate sauce,

marshmallow topping, chopped peanuts, toffee bits, sprinkles and maraschino cherries."

"I cweam?" Saige said hopefully.

Braden chuckled. "Yes, Cassie brought ice cream. And it sounds like a whole sundae bar, too," he noted, taking the bags and leading her through the living room.

Cassie shrugged. "I didn't know what you and Saige liked."

"What do you like?"

"Everything," she admitted.

He grinned. "A woman after my own heart."

But Cassie shook her head. "I'm only here for the ice cream." Then her gaze shifted, to take in the surroundings as she followed him toward the kitchen. "How long have you lived here?"

"Almost six years."

"So you've had time to paint—if you wanted to," she noted.

"Dana picked the colors," he admitted.

She squinted at the walls, as if looking for the color, and he chuckled.

"I know it's hard to see the difference, but the foyer is magnolia blossom—no, the original color was magnolia blossom," he remembered. "Now it's spring drizzle or summer mist or something like that, the living and dining rooms are vintage linen…I think, and the kitchen is French vanilla."

"In other words, every room is a different shade of white," she commented.

"Pretty much," he admitted, depositing the grocery bags on the counter so he could put Saige back in her high chair.

"I cweam!" Saige demanded.

"Yes, we're going to have ice cream," he promised.

His little girl clapped her hands together.

"Do you like chocolate sauce?" Cassie asked his daughter.

"Chay-wee."

"I brought some cherries, too," she said. Then, to Braden, "What I didn't bring was an ice-cream scoop."

He opened a drawer to retrieve the necessary implement, then reached into an overhead cupboard for bowls while she unpacked the bags.

"You should make Saige's sundae," she said, nudging the tub of vanilla ice cream toward him. "Because you know what she likes and what she can have."

"She likes everything, too," he told her. "Although she probably shouldn't have the toffee bits or peanuts. Or a lot of chocolate."

"Which is why you should do it," she said again.

So he scooped up a little bit of ice cream, added a drop of chocolate sauce, a dollop of marshmallow topping, a few sprinkles and three cherries on top.

"You need to use a spoon for this," he told Saige, setting the bowl in front of her.

"'Kay," she agreed, wrapping her fingers around the plastic handle of the utensil.

"How many scoops do you want?" Cassie asked him.

"How many can I have?"

She put three generous scoops of ice cream into the bowl, covered them with chocolate sauce, nuts, toffee bits, marshmallow topping, sprinkles and cherries. Then she prepared a second, much smaller bowl of the same for herself.

"I'm not sure why you came all this way to bring us dessert, but I'm glad you did," he told her, digging into his sundae.

"Bingeing on ice cream seems like one of those things that shouldn't be done alone."

"I seem to be the only one bingeing," he pointed out.

"And as good as this ice cream is, I can think of other and more satisfying things that shouldn't be done alone, either."

Her cheeks turned a pretty shade of pink as she dipped her spoon into her bowl.

"And maybe I wanted to have a real conversation with another human being as much as I was craving ice cream," she admitted.

"Conversation, huh?" He scooped up more ice cream. "That wasn't exactly what I had in mind, but okay. Anything in particular you want to talk about?"

"No." She slid her spoon between her lips, humming with pleasure as she closed her eyes. "Oh, this is good."

He knew she wasn't being deliberately provocative, but he recognized her expression as that of a woman lost in pure, sensual pleasure, and he found himself wishing that he'd been the one to put that look on her face. Because her blissful smile, combined with the sensual sound emanating from deep in her throat, had all of the blood draining from his head into his lap. To cool the heat pulsing in his veins, he shoved another spoonful of ice cream into his mouth.

"What did you have for dinner?" Braden asked, hoping that conversation would force her to open her eyes and stop making those noises that were making him aroused.

"A microwaveable chicken and rice bowl," she admitted.

"That sounds...incredibly unappealing," he decided.

She licked her spoon. "It wasn't that bad." And then she shrugged. "I do occasionally cook, but it's not a lot of fun to prepare meals for only one person."

"You can make dinner for me anytime," he told her.

"That's a generous offer," she said dryly.

He grinned. "I'm a generous guy."

"Hmm," was all Cassie said to that, as she spooned up more ice cream.

"Aw dun!" Saige announced.

He shifted his attention away from Cassie. "And it looks like you put more in your belly than on your face this time," he noted. "Good girl."

She smiled and rubbed her belly. "Mo?"

He shook his head. "No more ice cream for you or I'll never get you to sleep tonight."

"Chay-wee?" she said hopefully.

Before he could respond, Cassie had scooped one of the cherries out of her bowl and held her spoon out to Saige, who snagged the piece of fruit and popped it into her mouth. Then she smiled again, showing off the cherry caught between her front teeth, making Cassie laugh.

His attention shifted back to her, noted her curved lips and sparkling eyes. He'd always thought she was beautiful, but looking at her here now—in his kitchen, with his daughter—she almost took his breath away.

"Chay-wee?" Saige said again.

"I've got one more," Cassie said, this time looking to Braden for permission before she offered it.

He shrugged. At this point, he didn't think one more cherry was going to make any difference.

So Cassie gave Saige her last cherry, then pushed away from the table to clear away their empty bowls. While she was doing that, he got a washcloth to wipe off Saige's face and hands. He was returning the cloth to the sink just as Cassie closed the dishwasher and turned around, the action causing her breasts to brush against his chest.

She sucked in a breath and took half a step back—until she bumped against the counter. "Oh. Um. Sorry."

He held her gaze, watched her pupils dilate until there was only a narrow ring of dark chocolate around them. "Close quarters," he noted.

She looked around, managed a laugh. "This is not close quarters. You should see my kitchen."

"Is that an invitation?" he asked.

She tilted her head, as if considering. "Maybe."

He smiled and took a half step forward, so there was barely a breath between them. "I think we're making progress."

The tip of her tongue swept over her bottom lip, leaving it glistening with moisture. "Are we?"

He dipped his head, so that his mouth hovered above hers. "I haven't stopped thinking about our first kiss," he admitted.

"First implies the beginning of a series," she pointed out.

He'd noticed that she had a habit of reciting definitions and facts when she was nervous. Apparently he was making her nervous; she was definitely making him aroused.

"Uh-huh," he agreed.

"And I haven't decided if there's going to be a second," she said, the breathless tone undercutting her denial.

"That's okay—because I have," he said, and brushed his lips against hers.

Her eyelids fluttered and had just started to drift shut when the phone rang.

She immediately drew back; he cursed under his breath but didn't move away.

"Aren't you going to answer that?" she asked him.

"If my choices are answering the phone or kissing you, I opt for door number two," he told her.

But when the phone rang again, she lifted her hands to his chest and pushed him away. "I need to get home," she said.

With a resigned sigh, he stepped back.

A cursory glance at the number on the display panel had a whole different kind of tension taking hold of him.

"I'm sorry," he said, "but I do have to answer this."

"Of course," she said easily.

Nothing was easy about the emotions that coursed through his system as he lifted the receiver to his ear. "Hello?"

"Hi, Mr. Garrett."

"Lindsay?"

"Yeah, it's me," she confirmed.

He hadn't heard from Saige's biological mother in months, and the last he'd heard, she was in London. The 330 exchange, though, was Ohio, which meant that she was back at her parents' house.

As endless thoughts and questions tumbled through his mind, he vaguely registered Cassie lifting a hand in a silent goodbye before she stepped out of the room and then, out the front door.

Chapter Nine

Cassie didn't hear from Braden again until Friday afternoon when he came into the library. She was guiding an elderly patron through the self-checkout process and showing her how to unlock the DVDs she wanted to borrow. He waited patiently until she was finished, pretending to peruse the books on the Rapid Reads shelf, but she felt him watching her, his gaze almost as tangible as a caress.

"Can I help you with something, Mr. Garrett?" she asked when Elsa Ackerley had gone.

"You could accept my apology," he said.

"What are you apologizing for?"

"Not having a chance to say good-night before you left the other night."

"You were obviously focused on your conversation with...what was her name?"

"Lindsay," he told her.

"Right—Lindsay." She kept her tone light, feigning an

indifference she didn't feel. Pretending it didn't bother her that less than a minute after his mouth had been hovering over hers and anticipation had been dancing in her veins, he'd forgotten she was even there as he gave his full and complete attention to *Lindsay*. Proving to Cassie, once again, how unreliable her instincts were when it came to the opposite sex.

"And it's not what you think," Braden said to her now.

"I'm not thinking anything," she lied.

He opened his mouth as if to say something else, then closed it again when Helen approached the desk. After retrieving the basket of recently returned DVDs, she steered her cart away again.

"Have dinner with me tonight and give me a chance to explain," he said when Helen had gone.

"You don't owe me any explanations," she assured him. "And I'm working until seven, anyway."

"Then you'll probably be hungry when you're done," he pointed out.

"Which is why I have a pork roast in my slow cooker at home." Although she hadn't been able to firm up plans with Irene and Jerry, she'd impulsively decided to cook the roast anyway, figuring she'd take the leftovers to her friend on the weekend.

"I was offering to take you out for dinner, but that sounds even better," he decided.

She blinked. "What?"

"Dinner at your place is an even better idea than going out."

"I didn't—"

But he'd already turned and walked away.

Cassie huffed out a breath as she watched him disappear through the door. She didn't know if she was more amused or exasperated that he'd so easily manipulated the situation to his advantage, but there was no doubt the man knew how to get what he wanted—though she was still uncertain about what he wanted from her.

And while the prospect of sharing a meal with Braden filled her with anticipation, she couldn't help but wonder if he only wrangled dinner with her because Lindsay had other plans.

He wasn't waiting outside the door when she left the library and he wasn't in the parking lot, either. Cassie exhaled a sigh as she headed toward home and told herself that she was relieved he'd changed his mind. But she was a little confused, too. Braden had deliberately twisted her words to suggest an invitation she'd never intended, and then he didn't even bother to follow up on it. Maybe she hadn't planned to invite him, but she still felt stood up.

She shook off the feeling that she refused to recognize as disappointment and focused on admiring the many colorful flowers that brightened her path as she walked to her modest one-and-a-half story home that was only a few blocks from the library. The spring season was evident in the sunny yellow jessamine, vibrant pink tulips, snowy bloodroot and bright purple irises, and she felt her mood lifting a little with every step.

Her steps slowed when she spotted an unfamiliar vehicle parked on the street in front of her house. A late model silver Mercedes sedan. And leaning against the hood of the car, looking ridiculously handsome, was Braden Garrett with a bottle of wine in one hand and a bouquet of flowers in the other.

He smiled when he saw her, and her resolve melted away like ice cubes in a glass of sweet tea on a hot summer day.

"You said you were cooking a pork roast," he said by

way of greeting. "And while some people claim that pork is the other white meat, you once mentioned that you preferred red wine so I picked up a bottle of my favorite Pinot Noir." He offered her the bouquet. "I also brought you flowers."

"Why?" she asked, unexpectedly moved by the commonplace gesture. Because commonplace or not, it had been a long time since any man had brought her flowers.

"It's been a long time since I've had a first date, but I always thought flowers were a nice gesture."

"This isn't a date," she told him.

"Then what is it?"

"It's you mooching my dinner."

"I offered to take you out," he reminded her.

She nodded in acknowledgment of the point. "And then you deliberately misinterpreted my refusal as an invitation."

"You weren't asking me to come here for a meal?" he asked, feigning surprise—albeit not very convincingly.

"The pork roast isn't anything fancy," she told him, as she unlocked the front door. "And there's nothing for dessert."

"No cheesecake?" he asked, disappointed.

She was helpless to prevent the smile that curved her lips. "Sorry—no."

"Well, I'm glad to be here, anyway," Braden said, following her into the house.

Waning rays of sunlight spilled through the tall windows that flanked the door, illuminating the natural stone floor. The walls in the entranceway were painted a warm shade of grayish blue and the wide trim was glossy and white.

He was barely inside the door when he felt an unexpected bump against his shin. "What the—" He glanced down to see a cat with pale gold fur rubbing against his pant leg. "You have a cat."

"Two actually." She glanced over her shoulder. "That's Buttercup. She's much more sociable than Westley."

It took him a minute to figure out why the names sounded familiar. "*The Princess Bride*?" he guessed, carefully stepping around the cat to follow her into the bright and airy kitchen.

She seemed surprised that he'd connected the names to the story. "You've read the book?"

He frowned. "It's a book?"

Cassie shook her head despairingly, but another smile tugged at the corners of her mouth. "It was a book long before it was a movie."

"I haven't read the book," he admitted, as he looked around to admire the maple cupboards, granite countertops and mosaic tile backsplash. "But it was a great movie."

"One of my favorites." She took a meat thermometer out of a drawer and lifted the lid of the slow cooker to check the temperature of the roast. "And the book was even better."

"You're a librarian—you probably have to say that."

"Why don't I lend it to you, then you can judge for yourself?" she suggested.

"Sure," he agreed. "Mmm...that smells really good."

"Hopefully it tastes as good," she said. "It's a new recipe I'm trying out."

"So I'm a guinea pig?" he teased.

"As a result of your own machinations," she reminded him.

"I'm here for the company more than the food, anyway." He looked over her shoulder and into the pot. "Are those parsnips?"

"You don't like parsnips?" she guessed.

"Actually, I do. And sweet potatoes, too," he said, chunks of which were also in the pot. "I just didn't think anyone other than my mother cooked them."

"How lucky that you decided to invite yourself to dinner tonight," she said dryly, replacing the lid.

He grinned. "I was just thinking the same thing."

"Why don't you open the wine while I take care of these flowers?"

"Corkscrew?"

She pointed. "Top drawer on the other side of the sink. Glasses are above the refrigerator."

While he was opening the bottle, she slipped out of the room. The cat stayed with him, winding between his legs and rubbing against him.

He glanced down at the ball of fur and remarked, "Well, at least one of the females here is friendly."

"She's an attention whore," Cassie told him, returning with a clear glass vase.

"Where's Westley?"

"Probably sleeping by the fireplace—he spends most of his day lazing in his bed until he hears his food being poured into his bowl." Setting the vase aside, she opened the door of the pantry and pulled out a bag. She carried it to an alcove beside the fridge, where he saw now there were two sets of bowls neatly aligned on mats, and crouched down to pour the food.

As the first pieces of kibble hit the bottom of the bowl, he heard a distant thump of paws hitting the floor then saw a streak of black and white shoot across the kitchen floor. The plaintive meow made Braden realize it wasn't his bowl that Cassie had filled first. Her attention diverted by her sibling's call, Buttercup padded over to her bowl and hunkered down to feast on her dinner while Westley waited for his own.

"I've never seen a cat reluctant to eat out of another animal's bowl," he noted.

"Neither of them does," she told him. "Which makes it easier for me when I need to put drops or supplements in their food, because I know they've each gotten the right amount."

"Did you train them to do that?"

She smiled at that. "You've obviously never tried to train a cat to do anything."

"I'm guessing the answer to my question is no."

"No," she confirmed. "It's just a lucky quirk of their personalities. Or maybe it has something to do with the fact that, as kittens, they were crammed into a boot box with four other siblings. Now they appreciate having their own space—not just their own bowls but their own litter boxes and beds." Although they usually curled up together in one or the other when it was time to go to sleep, because apparently even feline creatures preferred not to sleep alone.

"Six kittens and you only ended up with two?" he teased.

"I wanted to take them all," she admitted. "But I'm not yet ready to be known as the crazy old cat lady."

"You're too young to be old," he assured her.

She lifted a brow. "I notice you didn't dispute the 'crazy' part."

"I don't really know you well enough to make any assertions about your state of mind," he pointed out. Then, "So what happened to the other kittens?"

"Tanya—you met her at the Book & Bake Sale—took Fezzik, Mr. and Mrs. Bowman—regular patrons of the library—chose Vizzini, Mr. Osler—the old bachelor who lives across the street—wanted Inigo, and Megan—one of the librarian assistants—took Prince Humperdinck, but she just calls him Prince."

"You named them all," he guessed.

"I found them," she said logically.

"That seems fair," he agreed, watching as she snipped the stems of the flowers and set them in the vase she'd filled with water. She fussed a little with the colorful blooms, so he knew she liked them. A fact she further confirmed when she set the vase on the windowsill above the sink and said, "Thank you—they're beautiful."

"They are beautiful," he agreed. "That's why they made me think of you."

"You always have the right line, don't you?"

"Do I?" he asked, surprised. "Because I often feel a little tongue-tied around you."

"I find that hard to believe."

"It's true," he told her.

While Cassie sliced the meat, Braden set the table, following her directions to locate the plates and cutlery. Then they sat down together to eat the pork roast and vegetables and drink the delicious Pinot Noir he'd brought to go with the meal.

"You're not going to ask, are you?" Braden said, as he stabbed his fork into a chunk of sweet potato.

She shook her head. "It's none of my business."

"Well, I'm going to tell you anyway—Lindsay is Saige's birth mother."

"Oh." Of all the possible explanations he might have given, that one had never occurred to her.

"When Dana and I adopted Saige, we promised Lindsay that we would keep in touch. But not long after the papers were signed, she went to London to do a year of school there, and although I routinely sent photos and emails, I hadn't actually spoken to her in more than a year."

"Why was she calling?" Cassie asked curiously.

"Because she's back in the US and wants to see Saige."

"Oh," she said again. "How do you feel about that?"

"Obligated," he admitted. "We agreed to an open adoption—of course, we would have agreed to almost anything to convince Lindsay to sign the papers—so I can't really refuse. And I do think it is important for Saige to know the woman who gave birth to her, but I'm a little concerned, too."

"About?" she prompted gently.

He picked up his glass of wine but didn't drink; he only stared into it. "Lindsay gave up her baby because she wanted her to be raised in a traditional family with two parents who would love her and care for her. And now that I'm a single parent, I can't help worrying that Lindsay will decide she wants Saige back."

She considered that as she sipped her wine. "I don't know much about adoption laws, but I would think it's a little late for her to change her mind, isn't it?"

"Most likely," he acknowledged. "The first thing I did when I hung up the phone after talking to Lindsay was call my cousin, who's a lawyer. Jackson assured me that judges generally don't like to reverse adoptions. But he also warned me that if Lindsay decided to take it to court and got a sympathetic judge, she *might* be able to claim a material change in circumstances and argue that Saige's best interests would be served by vacating our contract."

Cassie immediately shook her head, horrified by the possibility. "There's no way anybody who has ever seen you with your daughter would believe it's in her best interests to be anywhere but with you."

He managed a smile at that. "I appreciate the vote of confidence."

His smile did funny things to her insides—or maybe she was hungry. She decided to stop talking and start eating.

Braden's plate was almost empty before he spoke again. "Tell me something about you," he said.

"What do you want to know?"

"Have you been dating anyone—other than Darius Richmond—recently?"

She shook her head. "No. In fact, until a few months ago, I hadn't dated at all in a couple of years."

"Bad break-up before that?" he asked sympathetically.

But she shook her head. "The break-up was good—the relationship was bad."

His dark green eyes took on a dangerous gleam. "Was he abusive?"

"No, nothing that dramatic," she assured him. "I was twenty-six when I met him and eager to move on to the next stage in my life."

"Marriage," he guessed.

She nodded. "And kids. I wanted so desperately to get married and start a family that I saw what I wanted to see…right up until the minute the truth slapped me in the face—figuratively speaking."

"Were you married?"

"No," she said again. "Just engaged for a few months."

She thought back to that blissful moment when Joel Langdon proposed. They'd quickly set the date for their wedding and booked the church and the reception venue, and she'd been so excited for their future together, believing they were on their way to happily-ever-after.

"Until I discovered that he was still in love with his ex-wife," she continued.

Braden winced. "How did that happen?"

"As we talked about the wedding, I realized that Joel had some specific ideas about how he wanted his bride to look. A strapless dress wasn't appropriate for a church wedding, white satin would make my skin look pasty, and the princess-style ball gown would overwhelm my frame.

Instead, he'd suggested a more streamlined style, perhaps ivory in color with long sleeves covered in ecru lace."

"That's pretty specific," he noted.

She nodded. And although she'd been disappointed by her fiancé's assessment, she'd been pleased he was taking such an interest in the details of their special day.

"He also suggested that I should let my hair grow out, so that I could wear it up under my veil—but I hadn't planned to wear a veil. And maybe I could consider adding a few blond highlights, to tone down the auburn. The more suggestions he made, the more I realized that he was trying to change who I was—or at least how I looked."

She shook her head, lamenting her own foolishness for not seeing then what was so obvious to her now. She knew he'd been married before, but Joel hadn't talked about his ex-wife. He certainly never said or did anything to suggest to Cassie that he was still in love with her.

"It was only after I moved in with him that I found his wedding album with the date engraved on the front—the same month and day he'd chosen to marry me."

And the date had been *his* choice. She'd thought that a fall wedding might be nice, but he'd urged her to consider spring, so that she could carry a bouquet of white tulips—her favorite flowers. She hadn't much thought about what flowers she wanted for the wedding, and while she wouldn't have said tulips were her favorite, she liked them well enough.

"Then I opened the cover and saw a picture of his ex-wife, in her long-sleeved lace gown with a bouquet of white tulips in her hand." She'd slowly turned the pages, trying to make sense of what she was seeing. "And on the last page, the close-up photo of the bride's and groom's hands revealed that my fiancé had proposed to me with his ex-wife's engagement ring.

"The rest of it I might have been able to ignore," she admitted. "But when I saw the diamond cluster on her finger—the same diamond cluster that was on my finger—I felt sick to my stomach.

"And when I confronted him about it, he didn't even try to deny it—he just said he'd paid a lot of money for the ring. So I took it off my finger and told him that I hoped the next woman he gave it to wouldn't mind being his second choice."

All of which was why she'd barely dated in the more than two years that had passed since her broken engagement. Because in the space of the few hours that had passed between finding the wedding album hidden in the back of her fiancé's closet and his return to the apartment, she'd been shocked—and a little scared—by some of the thoughts that had gone through her own mind.

During that time, she'd actually tried to convince herself that she was making the discovery of those photos into more than it needed to be. She'd even considered putting the album back and pretending that she'd never seen it, to let it go so they could move forward with their plans.

Because she'd been desperate to feel connected to someone, desperate to be part of a family again. Even aware that marriage to a man who was still in love with another woman didn't bode well for their long-term future together, her eagerness to be a wife and then a mother almost made her willing to overlook that fact. *Almost.*

In the end, it was this desperation to not be alone that made her rethink her plans. Her mother hadn't ever been able to find happiness or even contentment on her own. Not even her daughters had been enough for her. She'd needed to be with a man; she'd needed his adoration and approval to justify her existence. The possibility that she might be like her mother—that she could make the same destructive choices and ruin not only her own life but that of any children she might have in the future—compelled her to take that step back.

Actually, she'd taken a lot of steps back. For a long time after she'd given Joel back the ring, she'd been afraid to even go out on a date. Her desperation to be a wife and a mother had made her question her own judgment and fear her own motivations. Thankfully, she had her job at the library to give her another focus, and she found both pleasure and fulfillment in working with children and teens.

She'd vowed then not to waste any more time with the wrong men. Unfortunately, the wrong men didn't always come with a warning label, as her recent experience with Darius Richmond had demonstrated. And if she wanted to find the right man, she had to be open to meeting new people.

Over the past few months, she'd started to do that, but none of the guys she'd gone out with had made her think "maybe this one." None of their good-night kisses had made her pulse race and her heart pound. In fact, none of their kisses made her want a second date.

No one had made her want anything more—until Braden kissed her.

Chapter Ten

"Cassie?"

She glanced up to find Braden watching her, his expression one of concern. She forced a smile. "Sorry—my mind just wandered off for a moment."

"How long ago was it that you gave him back the ring?" he wondered.

"Two years."

He set his cutlery on his empty plate and swallowed the last of the wine in his glass. "Did you live with him here?"

"No," she said again, smiling a little at this happier memory as she pushed away from the table to begin the cleanup. "I found this place when Stacey and I spent most of a rainy Sunday afternoon going through open houses. I think this was the third—or maybe the fourth—house we saw, and as soon as I saw the den with the fireplace and the built-in bookcases, I wanted it."

"I think I need to see the den," he remarked.

So she led the way through the dining room to her favorite room in the house. As he stepped inside, she tried to see it through his eyes. She knew it was modestly sized, as was the rest of the house, but there wasn't anything else about the room that she would change. Not the hardwood floors or the natural stone fireplace or the trio of tall narrow windows—each with a cushy seat from which she could enjoy the view of her postage-stamp-sized backyard—and especially not the floor-to-ceiling bookcases that covered most of three walls and were filled with her books.

"Well, it doesn't look as if you'd ever run out of reading material." He ventured farther into the room to examine the array of titles that filled her shelves and reflected her eclectic taste. From Jane Austen's *Pride and Prejudice* to J.R. Ward's *Dark Lover*; from Anthony Burgess's *A Clockwork Orange* to Shel Silverstein's *The Giving Tree*; from John Douglas's *Mindhunter* to Eckhart Tolle's *The Power of Now*. There were also biographies of historical figures, entrepreneurs and movie stars; books about auto mechanics and dogs and feng shui. "You have almost as many books here as there are at the library."

"Hardly."

"How many have you actually read?" he wondered.

"All of them—except for that bottom shelf," she said, pointing. "Those are new."

"You've read every other book on these shelves?" he asked, incredulous.

"Some of them more than once." She moved to the other side of the room and reached up to the third shelf. "Do you want to borrow this one?"

He took the book from her hand and glanced at the cover. "*The Princess Bride: S. Morgenstern's Classic Tale of True Love and High Adventure* by William Goldman."

He frowned. "Who's the author—Morgenstern or Goldman?"

She just smiled. "Read the book."

They returned to the kitchen and the task of cleaning up. "I'm sorry I don't have anything for dessert," she said.

"But you weren't expecting company," he said, speaking the words before she could.

"I guess I've made the point a few times."

"A few," he acknowledged, starting to load the dishwasher while she packed the rest of the meat and vegetables into a plastic container. "I'm still not sorry that I crashed your dinner party for one."

"I'm not sorry you did, either," she said, lifting her glass to her lips. "This is good wine."

He smiled. "I didn't think you'd admit that."

"That I like the wine?"

"That you like my company."

She opened the refrigerator to put the leftovers inside. "I never said that."

He chuckled as he closed the dishwasher. "I was reading between the lines."

She put the stoneware from the slow cooker in the sink and filled it with soapy water, then dried her hands on a towel.

When she turned away from the sink, he was right in front of her, trapping her between the counter and his body. *Déjà vu*, she thought. And in her kitchen, they really were in close quarters.

Braden lowered his head toward her. She went still, completely and perfectly still, as his lips moved closer to her own. Then he shifted direction, his mouth skimming over her jaw instead. The unexpected—and unexpectedly sensual caress—made her breath catch in her throat, then shudder out between her lips.

"Wh-what are you doing?"

"Well—" his mouth moved toward her ear, nibbled on the lobe "—you said there wasn't anything for dessert, and I was in the mood for something sweet."

Lust pulsed through her body, a relentless and throbbing ache. "And you think I'm...sweet?"

"I think you are incredibly sweet," he told her, his mouth skimming leisurely down her throat.

"Um—" she had no idea what to say to that "—thank you?"

She felt him smile, his lips curving against the ultra-sensitive spot between her neck and collarbone. "You really have no idea how you affect me, do you?"

"I know how you affect me," she admitted.

"Tell me," he suggested, his mouth returning to brush lightly over hers.

"You make me feel things I haven't felt in a very long time."

His lips feathered across her cheekbone. "What kind of things?"

Her fingers dug into his shoulders. "Hot. Needy. Weak."

"You make me feel all of those things, too," he assured her.

"When you kiss me...when you touch me...you make me forget all the reasons this is a bad idea."

He put his hands on her hips and lifted her onto the counter so that they were at eye level. He spread her thighs and stepped between them. "So maybe this isn't such a bad idea," he suggested, then covered her mouth again.

As if of their own volition, her legs wrapped around him, drawing him closer. So close that she could feel the ridge of his arousal beneath his zipper. She pressed shamelessly against him, wanting to feel his hardness against her. Inside her.

His hands slipped under her top, skimming up her belly to her breasts. She couldn't remember what kind of underwear she'd put on that morning—whether it was cotton or satin or lace. Lace, she decided, as his thumbs brushed over the nipples through the whisper-thin fabric, sending sharp arrows of sensation from the beaded tips to her core.

He made her want with an intensity and desperation that she'd never experienced before. Even in high school, when many of the other girls were slaves to their hormones, she'd spent most nights at home, alone. She'd been the quiet girl, the geeky girl. Most of the boys hadn't looked at her twice. She was too smart and flat-chested to warrant their notice. And that was okay—because she didn't want to be distracted from her plans and she especially didn't want to be like her mother.

She imagined that Braden had been one of the popular boys. Smart and rich and devastatingly good-looking. He certainly kissed like a man who had a lot of experience. And he knew just where and how to touch her so that her only thoughts were *yes* and *more*.

He was the type of guy who'd dated the most popular girls—the cheerleaders or varsity athletes. The type who never would have noticed her. And although they weren't in high school now, he was the CEO of a national corporation and she was a small-town librarian. In other words, he was still way out of her league.

But somehow, by some twist of fate, he was here with her now. Kissing her and touching her, and she was incredibly, almost unbearably, aroused. "Braden—"

He clamped his hands on the edge of the countertop and drew in a deep breath. "You want me to stop?"

She should say yes. She should shout it at the top of her lungs. What was happening between them was too much, too fast. She hadn't known him long and she certainly didn't know him well, but she knew that she wanted him and she hadn't felt such an immediate and intense attraction to a man in a very long time.

"Cassie?" he prompted.

"No." She shook her head. "I don't want you to stop."

"Tell me what you do want."

She lifted her eyes to his. "I want you to take me to bed."

The library had been Cassie's absolute favorite room in the house when she bought it, but since she'd converted the attic to a master bedroom suite, that had become a close second. The deeply sloped ceilings and dormer-style windows created a bright and cozy space that was, in her mind, the perfect place to snuggle under the covers.

To Braden, who stood about six inches taller than her, the space probably felt a little cramped. But he didn't complain when she led him up the narrow stairs and over to the queen-size four-poster bed set up in the middle of the room. Of course, that might have been because his mouth was preoccupied with other matters—namely kissing her senseless.

And his hands, those wide and strong hands, were touching her in all the right places, further heating the blood that coursed through her veins. He found the tiny zipper at the back of her skirt with no trouble at all, and then the skirt itself was on the floor at her feet. Less than a minute later, her blouse had joined it, leaving her clad in only a pale pink bra and matching bikini panties.

She wanted to touch him, too, but her fingers fumbled as they attempted to unfasten the buttons of his shirt. She'd only worked her way through half of them when he eased his lips from hers long enough to yank the garment over his head and toss it aside. Then her hands were sliding over warm, taut skin and deliciously sculpted muscles. He was so strong, so male, so perfect.

He hooked his fingers in the straps of her bra and tugged them down her arms as he skimmed kisses down her throat, across her collarbone. Then the front clasp of her bra was undone and he slowly peeled back the cups. She bit down on her tongue to prevent herself from apologizing for the small size of her breasts, because Braden didn't seem to have any complaints. And when his thumbs scraped over the nipples…*ohmy*, the frissons that sparked through her body.

Then he lowered his head to continue his exploration, and her own fell back as pleasure coursed through her body. He teased her with his tongue and his teeth, and when he took her breast in his mouth and suckled, her knees almost gave way.

He must have felt her tremble, because he eased her back onto the bed, and she drew him down with her. Though he was still half-dressed, she automatically parted her legs to fit him between them. His arousal was unmistakable and as her hips tilted instinctively to meet his, the glorious friction of the thick denim against the wisp of lace caused a soft, needy moan to escape from between her lips.

He pulled away from her just long enough to shed the rest of his clothes, then yanked her panties over her hips and tossed them aside, too. She wiggled higher up on the mattress, so that her head was cushioned on the mountain of pillows and so that his legs wouldn't be hanging off the end. He rejoined her on the bed and his mouth came down on hers again. Stealing a kiss. Stealing her breath.

If she'd thought about it, she would have come up with all kinds of reasons that this shouldn't happen. But with his mouth on hers and his hands stroking over her body, rational thought was impossible. Even coherent speech seemed beyond her grasp as she responded with only throaty sighs and needy whimpers.

And then, one desperate word, as common sense nudged its way into the middle of her true-life erotic fantasy.

"Condom," she gasped.

He groaned. "I don't have one."

Which probably wasn't surprising considering that he'd been married for so many years and, by his own admission, celibate in the year since his wife had died. Thankfully, she'd prepared for this possibility, remote though it had seemed at the time when she'd hidden the box of condoms among a variety of other items she'd purchased from the pharmacy.

"Top drawer of the night table."

He yanked open the drawer and found the box, tearing it open in his haste and scattering the strips of condoms all over the floor.

He swore; she giggled.

Finally, he had one of the little square packets in hand. Cassie tried to take it from him, but he held it out of reach.

"Not this time," he said. "I'm afraid if you touch me now, it will be over before we even get started."

"I think we've started," she said. "I'm so ready for you, I feel as if I'm going to explode."

"Sounds promising." He covered himself with the latex sheath, then parted her thighs and drove into her in one smooth thrust that made her cry out with pleasure.

Braden groaned his assent. "This…being inside of you… is even more incredible than I imagined."

Her cheeks flushed with pleasure. "You've imagined this?"

"Every night since I met you," he admitted.

She tilted her pelvis, pulling him even deeper. "So what happens next?"

He proceeded to tell her, in raw and graphic detail, how he wanted to pleasure her body. His words both shocked and aroused her, further heightening her anticipation. When he stopped talking, he focused his attention on doing everything that he'd promised. And it was exactly what she'd needed—and so much more.

When he was able to summon enough energy to move, Braden rolled off Cassie and onto his back. Now that blood flow had been restored to his brain, his mind was going in a dozen different directions. "I think we just shattered the world record for fastest simultaneous orgasms."

A surprised laugh bubbled out of her. "I feel so proud."

"You feel so good," he said, tightening his arms around her.

"If I'd had even an inkling that this might happen tonight, I would never have let you into my house," she told him.

"I didn't plan this. If I had, I would have been prepared," he said. "But I'm not the least bit sorry."

"Right now, I'm not sorry, either," she admitted.

It had been nearly a decade since he'd made love with a woman who wasn't his wife, and he'd expected to feel a little bit guilty after doing so. Regardless of the fact that his relationship with Dana had been deteriorating over the past several years, she'd still been his wife. But the minute he'd taken Cassie in his arms, all thoughts of Dana had been swept from his mind.

From the first moment that his lips touched hers, he hadn't thought of anyone but Cassie. He hadn't wanted anyone but Cassie.

"So where do we go from here?"

She nudged him toward the edge of the mattress. "You need to go home."

He didn't know whether to be insulted or amused by her ineffectual efforts to push him out of her bed. "You're kicking me out?"

"Don't you have to pick up Saige from your parents' house?"

He shook his head. "She's sleeping over tonight."

"Oh."

He slid his arm up her back and drew her closer. "Why are you so determined to draw lines and boundaries around what's happening between us?"

"Because if I don't, I'll try to turn this into something that it isn't," she admitted.

"Something like what?" he asked curiously.

"Like a happily-ever-after fantasy."

The admission gave him pause. Because he liked Cassie— and he *really* liked making love with Cassie—but he had no intention of falling in love with her. "You don't believe we can have a mutually satisfying physical relationship without making a big deal out of it?"

"I know that a couple of orgasms are not the foundation of a lasting relationship—"

"Three," he interjected. Then, in response to her blank look, he clarified. "You had three orgasms."

She blushed but didn't dispute his count. "The number is irrelevant. You have to—"

He silenced her words with a quick kiss. "Hold that thought."

She frowned at the command but didn't say anything else when he slipped from her bed. He'd noticed the small three-piece bathroom tucked near the stairs when she led him up to her bedroom. Thinking only of the necessity of dispensing with the condom, he wasn't paying attention to the shape of the space and, when he turned, rapped his head smartly on the sloped ceiling.

When he returned to the bedroom, rubbing his head, he saw that Cassie had wrapped herself in a short, silky robe and had scooped up the condoms that were scattered on the floor and stuffed them back into the broken box. He caught the edge of the drawer as it was closing and withdrew a strip from the box to set it on top of the table.

She looked at him, the arch of her brow as much a challenge as a question.

"I want to see if we can set another record," he told her. "For the world's slowest simultaneous orgasms this time."

"I'm not sure there really is such a record," she said dubiously.

"I don't care," he admitted. "I want to make love with you again."

Make love.

Those two little words stirred something inside of Cassie's heart. She was probably reading too much into the expression, especially considering that she would have been offended if he'd used the common crude vernacular. Still, there were other ways to describe the act, various euphemisms that he might have relied upon—such as the "mutually satisfying physical relationship" he'd already referenced. But she wanted to believe that what they'd shared was lovemaking, because she wanted to believe that hers wasn't the only heart involved in what was happening between them.

Except that she was trying to keep her heart *un*involved.

Yes, the experience of being naked with Braden had been beyond incredible, but she needed to maintain perspective here. He was a single father with a young daughter—a widower who had lost his wife barely a year earlier. It would be a mistake to believe that what they'd just shared was anything more than the result of an intense and mutual attraction or that it could lead to anything more than that.

"I have a habit of falling hard and fast," she admitted, as he eased her back down onto the mattress.

"Don't fall for me," he said. But with his lips skimming down her throat, and lower, it was really hard to concentrate on his words.

"I know I shouldn't," she acknowledged. "Because falling in love with a man who's still in love with the woman he married is a heartbreak waiting to happen."

He lifted his head to look at her. "You think I'm still in love with my dead wife?"

"It's okay, I know—"

"No," he said. "You don't."

She frowned at the certainty in his tone as much as the interruption.

He took a moment to gather his thoughts before he finally said, "The truth is, I'm only a widower because my wife was involved in a fatal car accident before she could divorce me."

"What?" she said, unable to make sense of what he was telling her.

"A few weeks before the crash…Dana told me that she wanted to move out," he admitted.

She couldn't imagine why a woman—especially a new mother—would choose to break up her family. Unless her husband was abusive or unfaithful. And though she couldn't imagine Braden being guilty of either of those offences, she was obviously missing something. "But… why?"

"Things hadn't been good between us for a long time," he confided. "I thought it was the stress of not being able to have a baby, and maybe that was a contributing factor, but obviously there was more going on than I realized. Only six weeks after we brought Saige home, Dana decided she couldn't do it—that she didn't really want to be a mother after all."

Cassie was stunned. She didn't understand why anyone would pursue adoption unless they were desperate to have a baby—or how anyone, when finally given the incredible gift of a child to raise, would suddenly decide that they didn't want to be a parent. "Oh, Braden," she said, her tone filled with anguish for him and what he'd been through.

"I'm only telling you this so you know that I'm not still missing my dead wife. I did grieve that her life was cut so tragically short—and I grieved for the loss of the life that I thought we were building together. But the truth is, the love we'd shared died long before she did."

"I'm so sorry," she said.

"The point of sharing that sordid tale wasn't to elicit sympathy," he told her. "It was to let you know that I'm with you because I want to be with *you*, because I don't want anyone but you."

Her heart began to fill with cautious joy and tentative hope. "Then this isn't…a one-night stand?"

"I sincerely hope not," he said.

The simple and earnest words tugged at her, but she struggled to maintain her balance. Because there was still a lot of distance between "not a one-night stand" and "forever after" and it would be a mistake to believe otherwise.

He tipped her chin up and brushed his lips over hers. "Now can we stop talking and start taking advantage of the hours we have left in this night?"

She lifted her arms to link them behind his head. "You don't want to hear all of my deep dark secrets?" she teased, in an effort to lighten the mood.

"Everyone has secrets," he said. "But unless you have six previous lovers buried in your backyard, I don't need to know all of them right now."

"Not six previous lovers, only one."

He paused, just a beat. "You only had one previous lover?"

She smiled sweetly. "No, I only buried one in the back-yard."

His lips curved just before they settled on hers. "I'm willing to take my chances."

Chapter Eleven

Saturday dawned bright and sunny—a perfect day for a trip to Frazer's Butterfly Farm made even more perfect by the fact that Braden had persuaded Cassie to join him and Saige on their outing. As they toured the facility, his daughter was mesmerized by the graceful fluttering wings of the colorful insects and happy to watch them swoop and glide. When one landed on Braden's shoulder, he slowly bent down so that she could get a closer look. Saige's eyes grew wide and she clapped her hands excitedly.

Of course, the sudden movement and sharp noise startled the butterfly and it flew away again. But there were so many of them that it wasn't long before another one—and then two and three—ventured over to feed from the sugar paper Cassie carried in her hand. And while Saige obviously enjoyed watching them from a distance, she screamed like a banshee when one of them dared to land on the guardrail of her stroller.

But the winged creature didn't go far—flying away from Saige's stroller only to settle again on top of Cassie's head.

"I'm holding sugar paper in my hand—why do they keep landing on my head?" Cassie wondered.

"Because your hair smells like peaches," Braden noted.

"You think that's what's attracting the butterflies?" she asked skeptically.

"It's attracting me," he told her, dipping his head to nuzzle her ear.

Despite the warmth of the day, Cassie felt shivers trickle down her spine and goose bumps dance over her skin. She put a hand on his chest and pushed him away. Braden grinned but backed off—for now.

They walked through the education center, where they could view butterflies at various stages of development— from egg to larva to chrysalis to butterfly. They even got to see a butterfly emerging from its chrysalis. One of the expert guides advised them that it was about to happen, pointing out the wings clearly visible through the now-translucent casing and contrasting it to other encasements that were opaque and green in color. The emergence didn't take very long, and though Saige didn't really seem to understand what was happening, she was content to sit in her stroller and munch on some cereal O's while Braden and Cassie watched.

"I've never seen anything like this before," Braden admitted, as the butterfly unfurled its vibrant orange-and-black wings.

"It is incredible, isn't it?" she said.

"One of Saige's favorite stories is that one about the caterpillar that eats and eats and eats until it becomes a beautiful butterfly."

Of course, as a librarian, Cassie was familiar with the story. "She's probably disappointed to see these caterpillars aren't eating through cherry pie and lollipops."

"I think she's just enjoying being here," Braden countered. "But speaking of eating—are you hungry?"

"A little," Cassie admitted.

"Why don't we go find someplace to have our lunch?" he suggested.

"That sounds like a good idea to me."

So they made their way outside, where there were walking paths and gardens and picnic areas and play structures. As they followed along the path, Cassie noticed a trio of butterflies circling around the stroller. She leaned down beside the little girl to draw her attention to the pretty insects, only to discover that Saige was fast asleep.

"If she's tired, she can sleep anywhere, anytime," Braden told her.

Which she remembered from the first day he was with Saige at the library, when the little girl had fallen asleep in his arms. "It must be nice, to be that young and carefree, with no worries to keep you awake or interfere with happy dreams," she mused.

"What kind of worries keep you awake?" he asked, steering the stroller off the path and toward the dappled shade of a towering maple tree.

"Oh, just the usual," she said dismissively.

He took a blanket from beneath the stroller and spread it out on the grass. "Job? Bills? Family?"

Cassie helped him arrange the cover, then sat down on top of it, leaning back on her elbows and stretching out her legs. "Actually, I love my job, I live within my means and I don't have a family."

After checking on Saige to ensure that she was comfortable, he stretched out beside Cassie. "No one?"

She shook her head.

"I can't imagine what my life would be like without

my parents, brothers, aunts, uncles and cousins and their spouses and children," he said.

"You're lucky to have them," she noted. Then, "This is an unexpected side of you—I never would have guessed that you were the type to watch butterflies in the sky or eat lunch on the grass."

"It's a new side," he admitted. "I used to be focused on the business of Garrett Furniture almost to the exclusion of all else. And then, when Dana and I decided it was time to start a family, I shifted my focus to the business of having a baby."

"Sounds romantic," she said dryly.

He managed a wry smile. "It was at first. Candlelight dinners and midday trysts. But when nearly a year passed with no results, it became an endless succession of tests and doctor appointments and schedules."

"Did they ever figure out why she couldn't conceive?"

"She had a condition called anovulation. It's a pretty generic term with numerous possible causes and, depending on the origin, there are various treatment options, some of them highly successful. But not for Dana."

"I'm sorry," she said sincerely.

"It was a difficult time for both of us," he said. "And then, six months after we finally decided to pursue adoption, we got a call to meet Saige's mom."

"That must have been exciting."

"Exciting and daunting, because we knew that she was meeting with four other couples, too, in an effort to find the best home for her baby. Our odds were, at best, twenty percent, because there was always the possibility that she would decide none of the couples was suitable and expand her search.

"And then, even when she did choose us, we knew there was still a possibility that she might, at the last minute, change her mind about the adoption entirely and decide to keep her baby."

"I can only imagine what an emotional roller coaster that must have been."

He nodded. "We were so excited—and so afraid to admit that we were excited in case the baby that was finally so close at hand would be snatched out of our grasp." He looked at that baby stretched out and sleeping in her stroller now, and a smile touched the corners of his mouth. "Since she was born, not a single day has passed that I haven't thought about how incredibly lucky I am to have her in my life.

"But still, aside from the fact that I was getting a lot less sleep, my day-to-day life didn't change a lot. And I was pretty proud of myself that I managed to squeeze fatherhood into my busy schedule.

"Then, one morning when I was getting Saige dressed, she was looking at me and babbling nonsense and I saw something in her mouth. Actually two somethings. She'd cut her first teeth. Not that they looked much like teeth at that point—more like tiny little buds poking through her gums. But it suddenly struck me that those two teeth hadn't been there the day before. Except, when I thought about it, I couldn't say for certain that was true. It was a normal milestone in a baby's life—but it was huge to me because I'd almost missed it.

"That was when I forced myself to slow down a bit and vowed to not just appreciate but savor at least five minutes with my daughter every day."

"She's a lucky girl," Cassie said softly.

"I'm the lucky one," he insisted. "I just wish…"

"What do you wish?" she prompted.

"Lindsay said that she chose us because we could give her daughter what she couldn't—two parents."

"There was no way you could have known that your wife would die only a few months after Saige was born."

"But even if the accident had never happened, we wouldn't be together now," he reminded her. And he'd been devastated not just that Dana's senseless death obliterated any hope of a reconciliation, but because it meant he'd failed his daughter, that the family he'd promised to give to her wasn't ever going to exist.

Cassie touched a hand to his arm, a silent show of support.

"When I got to the hospital and talked to the officer who had responded to the accident scene and he told me what had happened, do you know what my first thought was?"

She shook her head.

"I thought, 'Thank God, the baby wasn't in the car with her.' Even through the shock of losing my wife, there was relief that Dana didn't have Saige with her when she was hit—that our baby was safe."

"And you feel guilty about that," she realized.

"Hell, yes," he admitted. "I'd just found out that my wife was dead and, instead of being grief-stricken, I was relieved."

"You weren't relieved that she'd died—you were relieved that you hadn't lost your child, too," Cassie pointed out gently.

Braden nodded, accepting that she was right. And he was grateful that he'd found the courage to tell her about the feelings he'd never been able to speak about before, because her understanding helped him to finally attain a small measure of peace.

Cassie gave his hand a reassuring squeeze.

"Now—you said something about food," she reminded him.

He unpacked the contents of the cooler: buns piled high

with meats and cheeses, carrot and celery sticks, seedless grapes and miniature chocolate chip cookies. There was even a bottle of sweet tea for them to share and a couple of juice boxes for Saige, paper plates and napkins—and antibacterial hand wipes.

"You sure know how to pack a picnic," Cassie remarked.

"There's nothing very complicated in here."

"Those cookies look homemade," she noted.

"Not by me."

"Your mom?" she guessed.

He nodded.

"Did you tell her that you'd invited me to spend the day with you and Saige?"

"No," he assured her. "The last thing I want to do is encourage my mother's matchmaking efforts."

Cassie smiled at that as she unwrapped a sandwich. "Are you sure that's what she's trying to do?"

"There's no way she would ever 'forget' Saige's sock monkey anywhere unless it was on purpose."

"And what do you think was her purpose?"

"To put you in my path—or attempt to."

"She did seem disappointed to learn I wasn't there when you showed up to get the monkey," she acknowledged, nibbling on her sandwich.

"And since that failed, I'm guessing her next move will be to invite you to dinner at her house—and then she'll invite me and Saige, too," he warned.

"Do you really think she'd be that obvious?"

"She thinks she's subtle," Braden told her. "She invited the neighbor's single granddaughter to my brother Justin's thirty-fifth birthday party because she felt it was time he met a nice girl and settled down."

"And how did that work out?"

"Not the way she'd planned. Of course, she didn't

know—no one knew—that he'd already hooked up with Avery by then. And since they're happily married now, my mother considers it a win, especially since they've given her another grandchild. But she wants lots of little ones running around, which is why she's turned her attention to me again."

Cassie popped a grape into her mouth. "And how do you feel about that?"

"Well, I certainly can't fault her taste," he said.

"I have a horrible track record with men," she confided. "I tend to fall hard and fast and always for the wrong guys. Megan thinks that's because I grew up without a dependable father figure."

"Because your dad died when you were young," he remembered.

"And because he was an Army Ranger who, even before he died, was gone a lot more than he was home."

"Do you remember much about him?"

"Not really," she admitted. "Mostly I remember my mom always being so excited when he was coming home. She'd make sure the house was clean from top to bottom, she'd buy a new outfit, spritz on her favorite perfume, cook his favorite foods. She'd even dress me up in my prettiest clothes and braid ribbons into my hair.

"I loved my dad, but I didn't know him. Even when he was home, he seemed so distant and unapproachable. Now I would probably say haunted, although back then I just thought he was grumpy. I didn't look forward to him coming home, because I always knew he would go away again. And when he did, my mom would cry for days.

"She was a true Southern belle," Cassie explained. "Born in Savannah and accustomed to the attention and adoration that were her reward in the beauty pageant circuit. From what I've been told, my father fell for her, hard and fast. They had a whirlwind courtship and married after knowing each other only three weeks.

"After he died, she dated a few other guys, but none of them stuck around for long. I think I was twelve when she met Ray—an Episcopalian minister, widowed, with two sons. Eric and Ray Jr.—we called him RJ. My mom was a widowed military spouse with two daughters. I think she had some kind of image of us being a modern day Brady Bunch."

"So you have a sister?" he prompted.

She shook her head and wrapped her sandwich up again, her gaze focused on the task. "Had. Amanda was four years younger than me, and only ten when she died."

"What happened?"

Cassie took a minute, carefully wiping her fingers on a napkin, sipping the sweet tea he'd poured for her. "She'd gone fishing with Eric and RJ—just out to the pond at the back of Ray's property. They didn't usually catch anything, but they would spend hours out there trying, anyway. Amanda loved to follow the boys around—" she shook her head, her eyes shining with unshed tears "—no, she loved to follow *me* around, to pepper me with questions about everything until I told her to get lost.

"She wanted me to play some kind of game with her… I don't even remember what it was…but I told her I was busy and suggested that she go bug the boys. So she did, and they gave her a fishing pole and let her tag along. And I stayed in the house, studying for a science test because I was barely holding on to an A-minus and I knew I wouldn't be able to get a scholarship if my grade dropped."

"You were thinking about scholarships in tenth grade?" he asked, not just because he was surprised by the fact but because the anguish in her voice warned him where the story was going and he wanted to give her the option of a detour.

"When you grow up with limited financial resources, you need to think about all other options," she told him matter-of-factly. Then she fell silent for a moment before she steered the conversation back onto its original path. "So Amanda went off with the boys and I went back to my books, grateful for the peace and quiet.

"It was a long time later before RJ came racing back to the house. Apparently Amanda caught a small sunfish and was leaning forward to pull it out of the water when she lost her balance and fell in. But she was a good swimmer, so the boys weren't worried at first. They just watched the surface of the water, waiting for her to come up." Her gaze dropped away, but not before he saw that tears were now trembling on the edge of her lashes.

"Mom and Ray weren't home, so I was the only one there when RJ came running back to the house. I jumped into the pond where they said she'd gone in, and I pulled her out of the water."

There was nothing he could say to ease the pain he heard in her voice, a pain he knew she still felt deep in her heart, so he only put his arms around her and held her tight.

"Eric called 9-1-1 while I tried to remember the basic CPR I'd been taught in my babysitting course, but I knew she was already gone."

"I'm so sorry, Cassie."

"I was devastated." The admission was barely a whisper. "But my mother...my mother never recovered from losing Amanda. I don't know if she blamed herself for not being there or if losing both a husband and a child proved to be too much for her.

"She started to drink, as if the alcohol might fill up the emptiness inside of her, and she didn't stop. Six months later, she was dead, too—hit by a car when she was walking home from the bar one night."

And as horrific as it must have been for her mother to have lost that husband and child, he could not begin to imagine how much worse it had been for Cassie to have lost her father, her sister and then her mother. He wondered how she'd survived the devastation—and marveled over the fact that she had.

"The police ruled it an accident, but I'm not so sure," she admitted. "Maybe she was so drunk that she unknowingly stumbled into the middle of the road—or maybe she saw the headlights and wanted to make the pain go away forever."

He didn't know what to say to that. He wanted to reassure her that no mother grieving the loss of one child would willingly abandon another, but he didn't really know what her mother's state of mind had been. Maybe she had been so focused on everything she'd lost, she couldn't see what she had left.

"Ray, regularly prone to fits of temper, was always angry after that. He was furious with my mother for leaving him—and for leaving him with another kid. He'd frequently used scripture not as a comfort but as a weapon, and after my mother died, it got even worse. I went to church every Sunday, and sat beside the boys as he pontificated about sin. But even at home, the preaching never stopped, and when the words stopped being enough to satisfy his rage…he started to use his hands."

"He hit you?"

"Not just me," she said quietly, then shrugged. "Although I was the usual target."

"Did you tell anyone?"

"Who was I going to tell? I had no one. My father, my sister, my mother…they were all gone."

Listening to her talk about the experience, he couldn't even imagine what she'd gone through, how she must have felt. He only knew how he felt right now—furious and impotent—and he knew that if he could, he would go back in time and use his own hands on her stepfather.

"Please tell me that somebody did something," he implored.

"I spent a lot of time at the library when I was in high school," she reminded him. "And there's not much that gets past Irene. She took me to the hospital so there would be a documented record of my bruises, which prompted interviews by the police and family services. Of course, Ray had alternate explanations for my injuries—not the least of which was that I was absentminded and clumsy, never paying attention to where I was going and walking into things.

"The police officer who came to talk to Ray was sympathetic to the twice-widowed father trying to raise a teenage stepdaughter who wouldn't listen to anything he said—as Ray described the situation. Family services took a slightly harder line, offering counseling and insisting that he take an anger management course."

Braden was incredulous. "They didn't remove you from the home?"

"He was a minister—a pillar of the community."

He shook his head. "Sometimes the system really sucks."

"Sometimes it does," she agreed. "But the next time he knocked me around, Irene insisted on taking me to church for the Sunday service, and she wouldn't let me cover up any of the bruises. After the service, she met with the church elders, who later suggested that Ray might benefit from a change of scenery and offered him a position in Oregon."

"They should have offered him a position in the chaplain's office at Central Prison."

She managed a small smile. "He might have preferred that. In his eyes, losing the church in Charisma—where both his father and grandfather had preached before him— was a harsher punishment than being behind bars."

"Not harsh enough," Braden insisted.

"So Ray went to Oregon, RJ and Eric went to live with their maternal grandparents and I was supposed to be placed in a group home."

"Why a group home?"

"Because not many foster parents want an angry and grieving teenager living under their roof," she explained. "But I got lucky. By some miracle, a woman came forward for consideration as a foster parent and she was willing to take in an older child. A few days later, I was placed in her care."

And though Cassie didn't mention the woman's name, Braden knew—and he realized that he had severely misjudged Irene Houlahan.

Chapter Twelve

Cassie enjoyed the time she spent with Braden and Saige at the Butterfly Farm, but she was glad to go home alone at the end of the day. She'd poured her heart out to him—told him things that she'd never told to anyone else. And she suspected he'd done the same when he'd revealed the personal details of his marriage.

Somehow, the sharing of confidences seemed more intimate even than the physical joining of their bodies. As a result, she needed some space and time to think about everything that had happened on the weekend—and how to categorize their relationship. Were they friends? Friends with benefits? More?

Did he want more?

Did she?

She had yet to answer that question in her own mind when he called Wednesday afternoon while she was still at the library.

"How about dinner at my place tonight?" he suggested.

"What are you making?"

"Shrimp and grits," he told her.

"Mmm… I haven't had shrimp and grits in…years," she admitted.

"Is that a yes to dinner?"

"That's a definite yes."

"What time do you want to eat?" he asked.

"I finish at four today, so anytime after is good," she told him.

"Our usual dinner time is six, so we'll stick with that," he decided. "Do you want us to pick you up?"

"No, I'll drive myself so that you don't have to drag Saige out again to take me home."

"Okay," he relented. "I'll see you tonight."

"I'll see you tonight," she confirmed, and disconnected the call.

"Who are you seeing tonight?" Megan asked curiously from behind her.

Cassie sighed. "There is absolutely no privacy around here."

"What do you expect in a *public* library?" her friend teased.

"Good point," she acknowledged.

"So?" Megan prompted. "Was that the very handsome and rich Braden Garrett on the phone?"

"Yes," she admitted.

"And what is the plan for tonight?"

"Dinner."

"At his place," her friend mused.

Cassie frowned. "How long were you listening?"

"Long enough to know that shrimp and grits are on the menu," her coworker admitted unapologetically. "But the real question is…what's for dessert?"

Of course, that inquiry made Cassie remember the night she hadn't offered Braden any dessert, when his craving for something sweet had led to him kissing her—and the kissing had led to her bedroom.

"Well, well, well." Megan folded her arms on the counter and grinned. "The man is certainly doing something right if that dreamy look in your eyes and the flush in your cheeks is any indication."

"It's not the big deal you're making it out to be," Cassie protested.

"But the two of you are…dating?"

"No." She wondered how her friend would respond if she said, "just sleeping together," but decided the shock value of the revelation wasn't worth the plethora of questions that would inevitably follow.

Her friend arched a brow. "Having dinner together sounds like a date to me."

"I'm having dinner with Braden *and his daughter.*"

Megan ignored the clarification. "And you and Braden have really hot chemistry together."

Cassie shook her head. "I never should have told you about that kiss."

"The way the temperature soars whenever he's around you, I'm thinking there's been more than that one kiss." Which proved that she'd been keeping a close eye when Braden visited the library to return books he'd borrowed and check out new ones.

"It doesn't matter how many kisses—" or how much more than kisses "—there have been," she told her.

"I'm just happy to see that you're putting out—I mean, putting yourself out there," Megan teased.

Cassie felt her cheeks burn. "I think I'm going to call him back and cancel."

"Don't you dare," her friend admonished.

"Why not?"

"Because in the end, we always regret the chances we didn't take."

She lifted her brows. "Why does that sound like 'quote of the day' relationship advice?"

"Maybe because I read it on Pinterest."

Cassie couldn't help smiling as she shook her head. "Isn't that Introduction to Social Media group waiting for you in the Chaucer Room?"

"I'm on my way. But remember," Megan said, as she headed away from the desk, "those who risk nothing often end up with nothing."

"Apparently you spend too much time on Pinterest."

"It's an addiction," her friend admitted. "But since I don't have a handsome man offering to make me dinner, I've only got a computer to go home to at night."

Of course, Megan disappeared before Cassie could respond, leaving her alone with her thoughts and concerns— and a niggling suspicion that her friend was right, and if she didn't take a chance with Braden, she might regret it.

But taking a chance required opening up her heart, and that was easier said than done. It wasn't just her failed engagement that made her reluctant to want to risk loving— and losing—again. In fact, her relationship with Joel was the least cause of concern to Cassie. Far more troubling was the fact that everyone she'd ever loved had left her in the end: her father, her sister, her mother and, yes, most recently her fiancé. Was it any wonder that she'd put up barriers around her heart when she found herself alone— again—after giving back Joel's ring?

Maybe she was a coward. Certainly she knew plenty of other people who had just as much reason to be wary but still found the courage to open up their hearts again. Like her coworker Stacey, who was thirty-nine years old,

twice divorced and finally about to become a mother for
the first time. Her first marriage had ended after only ten
months when her husband decided that he just didn't want
to be married anymore; her second marriage lasted for
almost ten years before she finally left her abusive partner. It had taken years of counseling for Stacey to move
on after that, but she'd finally done so, and she was bliss-
fully happy with her new spouse and excited about having a family with him.

Obviously Stacey was braver than Cassie. Because as
much as she wanted the happily-ever-after that her coworker had finally found, she was starting to suspect that
some people were just meant to be alone. And maybe that
was okay. Irene Houlahan was a perfect example of someone who'd never married or had any children of her own,
and she seemed perfectly content with her life.

But even Cassie had to admit that, after seeing Irene
in the company of Jerry Riordan these past few weeks,
her friend had seemed more than content—she'd seemed
happy. So maybe there was no harm in spending some
time with Braden and enjoying his company.

Besides he'd promised her shrimp and grits, and she
was hungry.

Cassie made a quick stop at home to feed the cats and
change her clothes, opting for a pair of jeans and a short-
sleeved knit sweater layered over a tank top because the
wrap-style dress she'd worn to work only required a tug
of the bow at her waist to come undone. And then, not
wanting to show up at his house empty-handed after he'd
brought wine and flowers for her, she made another quick
stop on the way to his Forrest Hill address.

The contemporary two-story brick home on Spruceside Crescent was set back from the road and surrounded

by large trees that gave the illusion of privacy despite the neighbors on each side. She pressed a finger to the bell, and heard the echo of a melodic chime that somehow suited the house and upscale neighborhood. He greeted her with a warm smile and a quick kiss, and it was only when he stepped carefully away from the door that she realized Saige was holding on to her father's pant leg.

The little girl tipped her head to peek around him and grinned at Cassie. "Hi."

"Hello, Saige."

"What's in the bag?" Braden asked curiously.

"It's for your daughter," she said, offering it to the little girl.

Saige reached her hand inside and pulled out the package of box cars. Not knowing what trains she had, Cassie had opted for the accessory cars that would attach to any of the engines. When the little girl realized what they were, her eyes grew wide.

"Ope!" she said, shoving the package at her daddy. "Ope!"

"Please," he reminded her.

"Ope, p'ease," she said obediently.

He tore open the package, freeing the box cars for his daughter.

"Now you say thank you to Cassie," he said, when he gave Saige the cars.

"Dan-koo," she piped up.

"You're very welcome," Cassie told her.

"P'ay?" Saige implored.

"You want me to play?"

The little girl nodded so vigorously her ponytails bounced up and down.

"I'd love to play, if your daddy doesn't need any help in the kitchen."

"I certainly wouldn't object to your company," he told Cassie, 'but if you'd rather play with Saige, that's okay with me."

So Cassie let Saige lead her to the living room where, in place of the coffee table she'd seen on her last visit, there was an enormous train table covered with curving tracks that went over bridges and through tunnels, winding this way and that with switches and turnouts and railway crossings, ascending pieces and risers, towers and moving cranes and even a roundhouse.

"Wow," Cassie said. "This is quite the setup."

"P'ay," Saige said again, setting her box cars on the track and linking them to the red engine—obviously her favorite.

She looked at the various engines and specialty cargo cars on the track. "What train do I get to play with?"

The little girl crinkled her forehead as she considered. She decided on a green engine and turned to hand it to Cassie, then abruptly changed her mind and set it back down again. Next she selected a blue engine, then put that one down again, too. At last she decided on an orange one.

"I'm guessing orange is not your favorite color," Cassie said.

Of course, Saige didn't respond. She was already engrossed in driving her engine and box cars around the track, halting obediently at a railway crossing as she steered a purple engine pulling a passenger coach through on another part of the track.

After about ten minutes, Cassie realized why it had been so difficult for the little girl to decide which engine to let her play with, because she took turns with all of them, hitching and unhitching box cars and cargo cars to each of them in turn as she did laps around the table. Cassie stayed near the quarry, using her engine to haul imaginary cargo from the work site to the storage shed—and moving out of Saige's way whenever she raced past with one of her engines, obviously driving an express and in a hurry to get wherever she was going.

"Who's hungry?" Braden asked, poking his head into the living room.

Saige responded by immediately abandoning her trains and racing to the kitchen.

"Your daughter's definitely worked up an appetite," Cassie told him.

"She loves that train table," he noted.

"Who wouldn't?" she agreed.

"Now to see if you love my shrimp and grits," he told her.

"Well, they smell delicious."

He had a bottle of his favorite Pinot Noir in his wine rack and though she protested that she had to drive home, he opened it, anyway. She decided she would have one glass and no more—because she didn't want to give herself any excuses for staying, no matter how much she wanted to.

Of course, the man himself was much more potent than any amount of alcohol, and the more time she spent with him the more time she wanted to spend with him. And after her first taste of the meal he'd prepared, she realized that he'd seriously understated his culinary capabilities. The flavors enticed her tongue—his shrimp and grits every bit as good as what her mother used to make.

"Is something wrong?" Braden asked.

"No," she immediately responded. "Why would you think that?"

"Because you stopped eating and started pushing your food around on your plate."

"This is really delicious," she assured him, stabbing her fork into a shrimp, and then popping it into her mouth.

"So where did your mind wander off to?"

She finished chewing, swallowed. "I was remembering the last time my mom made shrimp and grits."

"Good memories?" he prompted hopefully.

She nodded. "Very good."

He topped up her glass of wine.

"I'm driving," she reminded him.

"Eventually," he agreed.

She picked up her glass and took a tiny sip. "Your daughter is obviously a fan of your cooking," she remarked.

"Saige is a fan of food," he told her.

"You're lucky—some kids can be finicky eaters."

He nodded. "My cousin's daughter, Maura, was an incredibly finicky eater when she was little. For almost two years, she hardly ate anything more than chicken fingers, sweet potatoes—but only if they were in chunks, not mashed—and grapes."

"Well, at least she was getting some protein, vegetable and fruit," Cassie noted.

"True," he acknowledged. "And while Saige doesn't turn her nose up at too many things, I'm not sure how much food actually ends up *in* her rather than *on* her."

Cassie had noticed that the little girl's determination to feed herself resulted in a fair amount of food on her face, dribbled down her shirt and in her hair. "I'm guessing that bath time follows dinnertime."

"And you'd be right."

"Mo," Saige said, shoving her empty plate toward him.

"How about dessert?" Braden suggested, catching the plate as she pushed it over the edge of the high chair tray.

"Zert!" she agreed happily, clapping her sticky hands together.

"Cassie?" he prompted.

"I very rarely say no to dessert," she admitted. "But I don't think I could eat another bite."

"Not even a bite of lemon meringue pie?"

She groaned. "You do know how to tempt a girl."

He grinned. "Is that a yes?"

"It's an I wish but still no."

"Zert!" Saige demanded.

"Coming right up," Braden promised his daughter.

He carried the stack of dinner plates into the kitchen. Cassie wanted to help him clear up, but she didn't want to leave Saige unattended, so she stayed where she was and did her best to clean up the little girl with her napkin.

When Braden returned, she saw that he carried a wet cloth in addition to the bowl containing his daughter's dessert. He set the bowl on the table and pretended to look around for her. "Saige? Where are you?"

The little girl giggled.

He turned his head from left to right and back again. "I can hear her but I can't see her."

Saige giggled again.

"Wait a minute—" He held out the cloth, then swiped it over his daughter's face, scrubbing away the remnants of her dinner. "There you are. You were hiding behind all those cheesy grits."

Saige grinned as she held out her hands for him to clean, too, in what was obviously a post-dinner ritual. Braden complied, then set the bowl on her tray table.

The little girl's dessert was flavored gelatin cut into squares that she could easily pick up, and she immediately dipped her hand into the bowl.

"Apparently you are a man of many talents," Cassie noted.

Braden shook his head. "I can't take credit for dessert.

My mother made the Jell-O squares, and the pie that you said you don't want came from The Sweet Spot."

The downtown bakery he credited was legendary for its temperamental pastry chef—and its decadent desserts. "Now I'm really sorry I don't have room for pie."

"We can always have our dessert after."

"After what?" she asked warily, watching as Saige curled her fingers around a square and lifted it from the bowl to her mouth.

He smiled. "Whatever."

"Braden," Cassie began, but the rest of what she intended to say was forgotten as Saige held a second square of gelatin out to her in silent offering. "Oh...um...is that for me?"

"Zert," Saige told her.

"Well, there's always room for Jell-O, isn't there?" she said, and opened her mouth.

It was his own fault that he'd been caught unaware.

Braden had been so focused on enjoying the time that he was spending with Cassie—and watching Saige and Cassie together—that he'd forgotten about Lindsay's telephone call only a week and a half earlier. He'd forgotten that his happiness was like a precarious house of cards, and that an unexpected puff of air—or an unannounced visitor—could cause it to tumble down around him.

Saige was finishing up her Jell-O when the doorbell rang, and he left Cassie in the kitchen with his daughter while he responded to the summons.

He opened the door, and his heart stalled. "Lindsay."

"Hello, Mr. Garrett." A smile—quick and a little uncertain—immediately followed her greeting. "I'm sorry to drop by uninvited, but I've been driving around for hours, not sure if I was actually headed in this direction."

"Did you want to come in?"

She nodded. "I want to see Saige."

Braden stepped away from the door. "You know you're always welcome."

"I know that visitation was part of our original agreement— but a lot of things have changed since Saige was born. In fact…I'm getting married at the end of the summer."

"Congratulations."

"Thanks." She tucked her hands in her pockets and rocked back on her heels. "The thing is…"

Whatever else she intended to say was temporarily forgotten as her gaze moved past him, and he knew, even before he turned, that Cassie was there with Saige in her arms.

"There's your daddy," Cassie said, halting abruptly when she saw that he wasn't alone. "Oh, I'm sorry. I didn't realize you had company."

"This is Lindsay," he told her. "Saige's birth mother."

"Oh," she said again, her gaze shifting from Braden to Lindsay and back again. "Hi."

Lindsay returned the greeting stiffly.

"Da-da!" Saige, oblivious to the tension, lifted her arms to reach out to him, and Cassie transferred the baby to him.

Lindsay's tear-filled gaze followed the little girl. "She's grown so much," she said softly. "She's even bigger than she was in the photos you sent of her first birthday."

He nodded.

"I'm, um, going to finish up in the kitchen," Cassie said, backing away.

"Nanny?" Lindsay asked, when Cassie had gone.

"No." He set Saige on her feet by the train table and settled into a chair, then gestured for Lindsay to sit.

She perched on the edge of the sofa, her hands twisting the strap of her oversize purse as if she needed to keep them busy to prevent herself from reaching out to the little girl.

"Saige doesn't have a nanny. She's with me most of the time and, when I'm at work, my mom takes care of her."

"It's nice that your family helps out," Lindsay acknowledged, opening her purse now and withdrawing an envelope. "But a little girl needs a mother." Then she lifted her chin and handed the envelope to him. "And I *am* her mother."

Chapter Thirteen

Even before Braden opened the flap and pulled out the papers, he knew what he would find inside: an application to reverse Saige's adoption. And though he understood and even—to an extent—empathized with her position, he had to believe that the law was on his side. That belief was all that allowed him to maintain a semblance of calm when he was feeling anything but.

"Not according to the State of North Carolina," he finally responded to her claim, his tone gentle but firm.

"An adoption can be reversed," she insisted.

He slid the papers back into the envelope and set it on the table beside him. "Usually only with the consent of the adoptive parents."

She frowned at that.

"I don't know who's giving you legal advice, Lindsay, but I can assure you that no judge is going to overturn an adoption sixteen months after the fact."

"But what if it's in the best interests of the child?" she persisted.

"She hasn't seen you in more than a year," he pointed out. "Do you really think it would be in her best interests to be taken away from everything she knows, and everyone who loves her, and placed in your care just because there's a biological bond between you?"

Lindsay's lower lip quivered as her eyes filled with tears. "I love her, too."

"I know you do," he acknowledged. "That's why you wanted a better life for her than you could give her on your own."

"But I'm not on my own now. And when I told Charles that I had a child, why I gave her up, and about you now being a single parent to Saige, he said she would be better off with us."

"I appreciate that you're thinking about what's best for Saige," he said, "but I promise you, staying here—where she's lived her entire life and where she has the love and support of my extended family and with whom she's bonded emotionally—is the best thing for her."

Lindsay swiped at the tears that spilled onto her cheeks.

"Look at her, Lindsay," he instructed, though the young woman hadn't stopped doing that since Saige had entered the room. "Do you really want to tear her away from the only home she's ever known? The only parent she's ever known?"

She choked on a sob, the ragged sound drawing Saige's attention from her trains to her visitor.

"Choo-choo," she said, holding up her favorite red engine.

Lindsay sniffled. "That's a pretty awesome choo-choo," she said, and was rewarded with a beaming smile.

"P'ay?" Saige invited.

She dropped to her knees on the floor beside the table and reached for a green engine. Saige immediately snatched it away.

"Saige," he admonished softly. "What have I told you about sharing?"

She set the green engine on Braden's knee, indicating her willingness to share with her daddy, then selected a yellow engine from the track for the visitor.

Lindsay, apparently happy just to be interacting with the little girl, began to move it around the winding track.

"So...the woman in the kitchen," she said, glancing up at him through red-rimmed eyes. "Is it serious?"

He knew that the question didn't indicate a shift in the topic of their conversation but was actually an extension of it. And of course, the honest answer was that his relationship with Cassie was still too new to be categorized. However, he knew that response wouldn't assuage her concerns, so he gave her one that would. "Yes, it is."

Lindsay was quiet for a moment before she said, "Saige seems to like her."

"Saige adores Cassie—and the feeling is mutual."

She watched the little girl play for several more minutes. "She seems happy," she finally acknowledged. "Here. With you."

"She is happy," he confirmed.

Her eyes again filled with tears as she watched Saige abandon her trains and raise her arms toward Braden, a silent request to be picked up. He lifted her onto his lap, and she immediately rubbed her cheek against his shoulder and stuffed a thumb in her mouth.

"I guess I just needed to see her again, to know it was true," she admitted softly. "I thought maybe she needed me...but it's obvious that she doesn't."

"Not being needed isn't the same as not being wanted," he told her.

She seemed surprised by that. "You'd still be willing to let me visit?"

"That was always our agreement," he reminded her.

She managed a smile. "Maybe I knew what I was doing when I chose you for Saige."

"I like to think so."

"I'll talk to my lawyer about withdrawing the court application," she said.

"I'd appreciate that."

His daughter yawned and tipped her head back to look at him. "Kee?"

"You can have your monkey after your bath," he promised.

Lindsay blinked. "Monkey?"

He nodded. "The sock monkey you gave to her when she was born—she won't go to sleep without it."

This time, Lindsay's smile came more easily. "And she's obviously ready for sleep now," she decided. "So I should be going."

Braden rose from the chair with Saige in his arms. "Can you say bye-bye to Lindsay?"

"Bye-bye," she said, and yawned again.

After a brief hesitation, Linday stepped forward and touched her lips to Saige's cheek. "Night-night, sweetie."

"Bye-bye," the little girl repeated.

"I'll come back to visit again," Lindsay told him. "But next time, I'll call first."

Cassie was just putting the last pot away when Braden and Saige returned to the kitchen. "Where's Lindsay?"

"She's gone," Braden told her.

"That was a short visit," she said cautiously. "Is everything okay?"

"I hope so," he said. "We cleared the air about a few things while you were clearing up in here—so thank you."

Though she had a ton more questions about the young woman's obviously impromptu visit, she held them back, saying only, "Thank *you* for the delicious meal."

"Why don't you relax with a glass of wine now while I get this one—" he glanced at Saige "—bathed and ready for bed?"

"Can I help?"

"If you want, but I should warn you—the whole bathroom can become a splash zone."

"I won't melt," she assured him.

As Cassie followed Braden up the stairs, she saw that the monochromatic color scheme continued on the upper level. His house was beautiful but incredibly bland and she wondered why he hadn't made any changes to the decor since his wife's death. Of course, the little girl in his arms was probably the answer to that question—no doubt Saige kept him so busy that painting was the last thing on his mind. But she couldn't help but think his daughter would benefit from a little color being added to her surroundings.

So she was pleasantly surprised to see that Saige's bedroom was beautiful and colorful. The room was divided horizontally by white chair rail, with the lower part of the walls painted a rich amethyst color and the upper part done in pale turquoise. On the wall behind Saige's crib, her name had been painted in dark purple script with the dot above the *i* replaced by a butterfly. A kaleidoscope of butterflies in various shapes and sizes flew across the other three walls so that the overall effect was colorful and fun and perfect for a little girl.

"This is amazing," Cassie said, as she traced the outline of a butterfly and realized it wasn't a decal but hand-painted.

"My cousin, Jordyn, helped decorate in here."

"She's incredibly talented," she noted. "Of course, she is Jay Addison, the illustrator of graphic novels."

"How did—" He shook his head, realizing the answer even before he'd finished asking the question. "My mother."

Cassie nodded. "She was at the library when I was unpacking the latest installment of A. K. Channing's series."

"Apparently she spends a lot more time at the library than I ever realized."

"Some people golf, others knit, your mother likes to read." She noted the bookshelf above the little girl's dresser. "And she's obviously passed her love of books on to her granddaughter."

"Saige never goes to sleep without a story," he admitted.

"Wee?" his daughter echoed hopefully.

"*After* your bath."

Which turned out to involve a lot of plastic toys and plenty of splashing, resulting in a more exhausting and time-consuming process than Cassie had anticipated. When Saige was finally clean and dry and dressed for bed, Braden asked Cassie if she could keep an eye on the baby while he cleaned up the bathroom. She happily agreed.

"P'ay?" Saige said hopefully.

"No play," her father said firmly. "It's bedtime."

"Wee?"

"Yes, Daddy will read you a story in a little bit," he promised. "Why don't you let Cassie help you pick out a book?"

His daughter took Cassie's hand and led her across the room to the bookshelf. Apparently she knew what story she wanted, because as soon as Cassie lifted her up, she grabbed *Goodnight Moon* and hugged the book to her chest.

"Kee," Saige said.

"Hmm…you're going to have to help me with that one," Cassie said. At the Book & Bake Sale, the little girl had said "kee" when she wanted a cookie, but Cassie didn't think that was what she wanted now.

"Kee," she said again, stretching out her free hand toward her bed.

"Ahh, *mon*key," Cassie realized, plucking the toy out of the crib.

Saige took the monkey from her and hugged it to her chest, too.

"All set now?"

The little girl nodded, even as her mouth opened wide in a yawn.

Cassie carried her to the rocking chair by the window and sat down with the baby in her lap.

Saige looked toward the door. "Da-da?"

"He'll be finished up in a minute—after he wipes up all the water you splashed on the bathroom floor," Cassie guessed.

Saige responded by snuggling in to her embrace, the back of her head dropping against Cassie's shoulder. She lifted a fist—the one still clutching the sock monkey—to rub her eye.

"You're a sleepy girl, aren't you?"

Saige's only response was another yawn.

"Do you want me to read your story or are you waiting for Daddy?"

"Wee," Saige replied, offering her the book.

So Cassie took it from her hand and opened the cover. She began to read, not needing to look at the page to recite the words of the classic story she'd read aloud at the library more times than she could count.

And although it wasn't a long story, Saige's eyelids had

drifted shut before the little bunny had wished good night to half of the objects in the great green room. But Cassie read all the way to the last page before setting the book aside. Still, the baby didn't stir.

Cassie continued to sit with her, the weight of the little girl in her arms filling her heart and reminding her of the dreams she'd tried to put aside. Dreams that had teased and tempted for many years but so far remained unfulfilled.

Tonight, Braden had given her a glimpse of the life she'd always imagined in her future. A home, a husband, a family. It wasn't so much—and yet it was everything she'd always wanted. And being with Braden and Saige, she was tempted to let herself dream again. To believe that she might one day be part of a family again, maybe even *this* family.

Of course, she was getting way ahead of herself. She hadn't known Braden very long and didn't know him very well, and it would be foolish to hope that one night could lead to a lifetime together.

You can't start the next chapter of your life if you keep rereading the last one.

Great—not only was Megan quoting words of wisdom from Pinterest, now those words were echoing in the back of Cassie's head.

Maybe it was clichéd advice—and maybe it was true. Maybe it was her own past experiences that were preventing her from moving forward with her life. And maybe, if she let herself open her heart, she might discover that Braden and Saige weren't just characters in her next chapter but in every chapter of the rest of her life.

It didn't take Braden long to wipe out the tub and dry off Saige's toys, but when he made his way across the hall after completing those tasks, his daughter was already asleep. And in that moment, looking at Saige snuggled contentedly in Cassie's arms, he knew: she was the one.

Cassie was the perfect mother for his little girl—the mother that Saige deserved.

Now he only had to convince her of that fact.

He didn't think it would be too difficult. Cassie had admitted that she wanted to be a wife and a mother and, coincidentally, he needed a wife and a mother for his daughter. It was, from his perspective, a win-win.

The fact that he didn't—wouldn't—love her, didn't have to be a barrier to a future for them together. He could be a good husband—affectionate and faithful—without opening up his heart. And he would do everything in his power to make Cassie happy, to show her how much he appreciated her presence in their lives.

"I think you have the touch," he said, speaking quietly from the doorway.

"It doesn't require any special magic to get an exhausted child to sleep," Cassie pointed out.

"If you were ever here at two a.m., you'd know that's not true," he commented dryly.

"She doesn't sleep through the night yet?"

"Most nights she does," he acknowledged. "But lately she's decided that two a.m. is playtime. She doesn't wake up because she's wet or hungry, she just wants to play. And then, after being up for half the night, she has a three-hour nap at my mother's house."

"Fiona, one of the moms in Toddler Time, went through something like that with her little guy," Cassie told him. "He would sleep at day care but not at home. According to her pediatrician, it's not uncommon with babies who want to spend time with their working parents."

"Well, giving up my job isn't really an option," he noted.

"And my mom's trying to break her of the habit by limiting her naptime during the day."

"That might be why she fell asleep so easily tonight," Cassie noted.

"Or maybe you tired her out, making her chase all of those trains around the track."

"You're giving me too much credit," she told him.

He shook his head. "I don't think so. I've seen you with the kids at the library—from babies to teens," he reminded her. "You have an instinctive ability to empathize and relate to all of them."

"I love working with kids."

"Did that broken engagement destroy all hope of having your own?"

"No," she denied. "But I would like to have a husband before the kids and, so far, that hasn't worked out."

"Well, maybe you'll luck out someday and meet a fabulous guy who already has a child," he suggested. "Perhaps an adorable little girl."

"That would be lucky," Cassie said lightly.

"Or maybe you've already met him."

"Maybe I have," she acknowledged. "And maybe I specifically recall the fabulous guy with the adorable little girl warning me not to fall for him."

He leaned down to lift his sleeping daughter from her arms and touch his lips to Cassie's. "But that was before he started falling for you."

He tucked Saige into her crib, ensuring that her sock monkey was beside her, then he took Cassie's hand and led her back downstairs.

"Why don't you sit down by the fire?" he suggested. "I'll be there in just a sec."

She went into the living room, but when he returned with their glasses and the rest of the bottle of wine, he saw that she was standing by the fireplace, looking at the photographs lined up on the mantel. Several were of Saige, the rest were various other members of his family.

She set down the picture in her hand—a candid shot taken at Lauryn and Ryder's wedding—and accepted the wine he offered.

"It was big news when they got married," she commented. "A daughter of Charisma's most famous family stealing the heart of America's hottest handyman."

He nodded. "But not quite as big as when my brother Ryan married Harper, daughter of soap actor Peter Ross. We had actual paparazzi in town to cover that event."

"It really is a small world, isn't it?" she mused. "The first time I ever saw Ryder Wallace was on *Coffee Time with Caroline*, which was produced by your sister-in-law, and now he's married to your cousin."

"And his sister is married to my brother Justin."

"Apparently it's even smaller than I realized."

"Especially if you're a Garrett," Braden remarked. "I swear, I can't move in this town without bumping into someone I'm related to. And it will only get worse when Ryan and Harper move back from Florida and Lauryn and Ryder return from Georgia."

"But you don't really mind," Cassie guessed. "I can tell by all these photos—and your mother's stories—that your family is close."

"We are," he agreed. "As much as they drive me crazy at times, I don't know what I would do without them."

"I miss that," she admitted.

"Being driven crazy?"

She smiled as she shook her head. "Being part of a family."

"A Day with the Garrett Clan might cure you of that,"

he suggested. And if she didn't run screaming, that would be his cue to take the next step.

"A Day with the Garrett Clan sounds like an event you'd sell tickets to," she teased.

"Maybe I'll suggest that in advance of the next family gathering, but this one is an informal welcome home barbecue at my parents' place on Sunday for Ryan, Harper and Oliver. You should come."

"If the whole family is going to be there, I'm sure your parents won't want extra people underfoot."

"Are you kidding? My mother is happiest in complete chaos—and I know she'd be thrilled to see you there."

"Aren't you worried that she might make a big deal out of me being there with you?" she asked cautiously.

He grinned. "*Everyone* will make a big deal out of you being there with me."

"Are you trying to talk me *into* or *out of* going to this barbecue?"

"Into," he assured her. "I very much want you there with me. I want you to meet my family and I want them to meet you."

Still, she hesitated. "I just think it might be too soon."

"Why?"

"Because I have a really lousy track record with relationships," she admitted.

"Most people go through a few failed relationships before they figure out how to make it work—or even realize that they want to." He slid his arms around her, drawing her closer. "We can make this work, Cassie."

"Do you really think so—or are you just saying that to get me into bed again?"

"If I wanted to get you into bed again, I wouldn't waste my breath on words," he said.

"What would—" She shook her head. "Forget it. I don't want to know."

He dipped his head, but paused with his lips hovering just a fraction of an inch above hers. "I think you do want to know. And I think you really want me to kiss you."

She responded by lifting her chin to breach the scant distance and press her mouth to his.

He believed what he'd said to her—that they could make a relationship work—and the powerful chemistry between them was only one of the many reasons. And when she was in his arms, it was an unassailable reason.

He knew a relationship required more than physical attraction. Passion was the icing on the cake rather than the base layer, more decorative than essential. But it was also able to transform something good into something spectacular. And making love with Cassie was spectacular.

He liked who she was and everything about her. She was warm and kind and compassionate, beautiful and smart and funny. He enjoyed spending time with her, talking to her and making love with her—but he wasn't going to fall in love with her.

It wasn't just that he was unwilling to risk heartbreak again—it was that he didn't have anything left in his heart to give to anyone else. The failure of his marriage—and the sense that he had failed the woman he'd vowed to love, honor and cherish—had undoubtedly broken a piece of his heart. But only a piece, because the rest was filled with the pure love he felt for Saige, and he didn't want or need anything more than that.

But his daughter did, and he owed it to Saige to give her the life that her birth mother wanted for her. A real family. A whole family. He didn't believe Lindsay would ever be able to take Saige away—and hopefully, after their conversation today, she wouldn't even try—but he did agree that his little girl needed a mother. And he couldn't imagine a woman who would be more perfect for the role than the one he was kissing right now.

They were both breathless when she finally eased away from him. He lifted a finger to her chin, tilting her head back so that he could look into her beautiful dark eyes. "Will you stay with me tonight?" he asked.

"For a while," she agreed.

"That's a start," he said, and led her down the hall.

Chapter Fourteen

Cassie was in way over her head.

She knew it, and she didn't care. When she was with Braden, when his hands were on her body, it was difficult to care about anything but how good he made her feel. And he instinctively knew how to make her feel really good.

She'd never had a lover who was so closely attuned to the wants and needs of her body, but Braden was nothing if not attentive. He used her sighs and gasps and moans to guide his exploration of her body, and his own lips and his hands to lead her slowly and inexorably toward the ultimate pinnacle of pleasure.

She followed not just willingly but eagerly, their discarded clothing marking the path to his bedroom. Somewhere in the back of her mind, she knew that they were venturing into dangerous territory—but she didn't care. Her body already knew him and wanted him and her heart refused to heed the warnings of her mind.

His hands stroked down her back, over the curve of her bottom, drawing her closer. She touched her mouth to his chest, and let her tongue dart out to taste his skin. He tasted good. Hot. Salty. Sexy. She skimmed her lips down his breastbone, then flicked her tongue over his nipple, eliciting a low growl of approval. She reached down between their bodies as her mouth moved to his other nipple, and wrapped her hand around the rigid length of him. She felt him jerk against her palm, and was pleased to know that he wanted her as much as she wanted him.

She started to move lower, her mouth trailing kisses down his belly, but he caught her arms and hauled her up again, his tongue sliding deep into her mouth in a kiss that was so hot and hungry it made her head spin and her knees tremble.

She tumbled onto the mattress, dragging Braden down with her. He pulled away only long enough to sheathe himself with a condom, then he parted her thighs and thrust into her. She gasped with pleasure, instinctively tilting her hips so that they were joined as deeply and completely as possibly.

He filled all her senses. She could see nothing but the intensity of his deep green eyes locked with her own; hear nothing but the roar of blood through her veins; taste nothing but the sweetest passion when his mouth covered hers again; feel nothing but the most exquisite bliss as their bodies merged and mated and…finally…leaped over the precipice together.

She was still waiting for her heart to stop racing when she heard a soft sound somewhere in the distance. While she was attempting to decipher what it was and from where it had come, Braden was already sliding out from beneath the covers that he'd yanked up over their naked bodies sometime after they'd collapsed together.

"I'll be right back," he said, brushing a quick kiss over her lips, having shifted gears from lover to father in the blink of an eye.

A moment later, she heard the soft murmur of his voice through the baby monitor that she now realized was on the bedside table. She couldn't hear what he was saying, but his tone was soothing, reassuring.

A few minutes later, she heard his footsteps enter the room again. She lifted her arm away from her forehead and peeled open one eyelid—then the second, when she saw that he was carrying an enormous wedge of lemon meringue pie on a plate.

"I thought you went to check on Saige."

"I did. She's fine," he assured her. "But I thought you might be ready for dessert now."

"That's for me?"

"It's for both of us," he said.

She wiggled up to a sitting position, tucking the sheet under her armpits to ensure she was covered.

He grinned. "It's a little late for modesty, don't you think?"

"I'm not going to sit here naked and eat pie," she protested.

He shrugged, broke off the tip of the pie with the fork and held it toward her—then pulled it away and ate the bite himself.

She frowned.

"Mmm...this is really good. The lemon is the perfect balance of sweet and tart and the meringue—" he cut off another piece, popped it into his mouth "—is so incredibly light and fluffy."

"You said that was to share," she reminded him.

"You give up the sheet and I'll give you some pie."

"Seriously?"

"Those are my terms," he told her.

She hesitated; he took another bite of the pie.

Her mouth watered as she watched the fork slide between his lips, swallowing up the flaky crust, tart filling and fluffy meringue, and she decided he was right—it was a little late for modesty.

She dropped the sheet; he grinned. This time, when he scooped up a forkful of pie, he held it close for her to sample. She could smell it—the tangy sweet scent—just before she parted her lips to allow him to slide the fork into her mouth.

She closed her eyes and sighed with blissful pleasure. "Oh, yeah. This is really good."

He lifted the fork again, but the pie slid off the tines and onto her thigh, near her hip. She yelped. "That's cold."

"Sorry," he said, even as he lowered his head to clean up the dessert with his mouth. He licked her skin thoroughly, making her suspect that the mishap might not have been an accident after all.

"Two can play that game," she warned him, and scooped some of the meringue off the pie with her finger, then smeared it on his belly before cleaning it up with her mouth.

He retaliated by dabbing lemon filling on each of her nipples and suckling the rigid peaks until she was gasping and squirming.

And so they went back and forth, taking turns savoring the dessert from one another's bodies. Then they made love again, the remnants of the pie creating a sticky friction between them and necessitating a quick shower afterward.

A shower that ended up not being so quick, as the slow, sensual soaping of one another's bodies had their mutual passion escalating again. When Braden finally twisted the knob to shut off the spray, it had started to go cold, and they were still dripping with water when they tumbled onto his bed again.

As Cassie drifted to sleep in his arms, she realized that she'd gone and done what she'd promised herself she wouldn't: she'd fallen head over heels in love with Braden Garrett.

Braden's maternal grandmother had been a resident of Serenity Gardens for the last ten years of her life. Of course, she'd passed away more than a dozen years earlier and the residence had undergone significant renovations and benefitted from a major addition since then. Thankfully, the main reception desk was in the same place and, after buzzing up to Irene Houlahan's room, he and Saige were cleared to find their way to Room 508 in the North Wing.

When they arrived at her door, it was ajar. He remembered that his grandmother had often left her door open, too, to welcome any neighbors who wanted to drop in for a visit. Still, he knocked on the portal and waited for Miss Houlahan's invitation before pushing the door wider.

The old woman was seated at one end of an overstuffed sofa in the living room, a thick hardcover book open in her lap. The permanent furrow between her brows relaxed marginally when her gaze lit on his daughter by his side, and she closed her book and set it aside. "Hello, Saige."

His little girl didn't have a shy bone in her body, and while he hovered on the threshold, she happily toddled across the room to the sofa. Once there, she climbed up onto the cushions, surprising Braden as much as Irene when she pursed her lips and kissed the old woman's wrinkled cheek.

"Well," Irene said, as if she wasn't quite sure how to

respond to the gesture. "It's not often that I have the pleasure of such a young visitor." Then she lifted her gaze to
Braden's. "And since you're not the Grim Reaper, you can
come in, too."

He fought against a smile as he stepped farther into
the room.

"I don't imagine you were just 'in the neighborhood,'"
Irene said.

"Not really," he admitted, setting the vase on the table
beside the sofa. "We came to deliver these."

Saige, having noticed the stack of photo books on the
coffee table, slid off the sofa again and reached for the one
on top. Braden caught her hands and gently pried them
from the cover. "Those are Miss Houlahan's books—
they're not for little girls."

"I always believed books were intended to be read by
anyone who was interested," Irene contradicted him. "But
I don't imagine pictures of coffee tables would be of much
interest to a toddler."

Braden had been so focused on ensuring his daughter
didn't damage the item he hadn't taken note of the cover,
but he did now. "A coffee table book about coffee tables?"

"Cassie's idea of a joke." She shifted forward and removed a different book from the bottom of the pile: *A Vibrant History of Pop Art.*

"This has some strange stuff in it but at least the pictures are colorful," she told him. Then she turned to his
daughter and asked, "Do you want to look at this one?"

Saige nodded and Irene set the book on the table in front
of her, then opened it up to the middle. Saige lifted all of
the pages from the front cover and pushed them over so
that she could start at the front.

"She knows how to read a book," Irene noted.

"We read every night before bed, and my mother takes her to the library a couple of times a week."

"A child who reads will be an adult who thinks," the former librarian said approvingly. "Now tell me what the flowers are for, because I'm not so old that I've forgotten when my birthday is and I know it's not today."

"Why does there need to be an occasion?" he countered.

"Because I've never known a man to bring flowers to a woman without one."

"Then maybe you've known the wrong men," he told her.

"You're trying to sweeten me up so I'll say good things about you to Cassie, aren't you?" she guessed.

He suspected it would take a lot more than a bouquet of flowers to do that, but he bit down on his tongue to prevent the thought from becoming words. "No," he denied. "I'm trying to say thank you."

"For what?" she asked, obviously still suspicious.

"For being there for Cassie when no one else was."

She scowled. "I don't know what you think I did—"

"I think you saved her life."

Irene snorted. "I did nothing of the sort."

"I don't mean literally," he explained. "But she told me about everything that happened the year her sister—and then her mother—died."

Irene peered at him over the rim of her glasses, her gaze speculative. "Cassie doesn't often talk about her family," she noted.

"She also told me that you appealed to the church to have her stepfather sent away—and gave family services the evidence they needed to ensure that he couldn't take Cassie with him."

"I didn't realize that she knew anything about that," Irene admitted.

"And then, because you recognized that she was just as terrified of the system as she was of her abusive step-father, you took her into your home."

"It wasn't a sacrifice to give her an extra bedroom."

He glanced at Saige, who was braced on her arms on the table, leaning close to scrutinize the details in the pictures.

"You gave her more than that," he said to Irene. "You gave her security, guidance and direction. You helped her focus on and achieve her goals."

"I didn't do any of it for thanks," she told him.

"I know, but I'm thanking you, anyway."

"Well, it was a nice gesture," she admitted, just a little begrudgingly.

He held back his smile. "If you give me a chance, you might find that I'm a nice guy."

"Maybe I will," she conceded, with just the hint of a smile tugging at her mouth.

The next day, when Cassie was visiting Irene, she saw the vase of colorful blooms prominently displayed on the coffee table.

"I see Jerry brought you flowers again," she noted.

"Those aren't from Jerry," Irene told her.

"Really?" She grinned. "You have another suitor in competition for your affections?"

Her friend sniffed. "Not likely. Those are from *your* suitor."

Cassie lifted a brow.

"Braden Garrett came to see me yesterday."

"He did?"

Irene nodded. "Brought his little girl with him—goodness, she's just a bundle of sweetness and joy, isn't she?"

"Saige is a very happy child," Cassie agreed.

"You've been spending a lot of time with them lately?"

"I guess I have," she agreed cautiously.

"A man like that, with a young child to raise, is a package deal," Irene warned her.

"I know."

"And you love them both already, don't you?"

There was no point in telling the old woman it wasn't any of her business. When Irene had taken an angry and grieving fifteen-year-old girl into her home, Cassie's business had become her business. Since that time, she'd been Cassie's legal guardian and surrogate mother, and she'd never hesitated to ask Irene for guidance and advice when she needed it. In the current situation, she decided that she needed it because her feelings for Braden and Saige had become so muddled with her own hopes and dreams that she feared she'd lost perspective.

"I do," she admitted.

"Why don't you sound happy about it?"

"Because I didn't want to fall in love with Braden," she admitted. "I didn't want to give him the power to break my heart."

"Loving someone is always a risk," Irene acknowledged.

"Please don't start quoting Pinterest advice to me."

"You don't need any advice—you just need to follow your heart."

"Because that's never steered me wrong in the past," Cassie noted dryly.

"Stop dwelling on the past and focus on the future," her friend suggested.

"That definitely sounds like Pinterest advice."

Irene handed Cassie the book she'd been reading during her previous visit.

"There's a lot of good stuff on Pinterest," she said. "But not a lot of men like Braden Garrett in the world."

* * *

Maybe Cassie should have made an excuse to get out of attending the welcome home party for Braden's brother and sister-in-law, but she was curious to see him interact with the whole family, and she wanted to be able to tell Megan—who was a huge fan of *Ryder to the Rescue*—that she'd met Ryder Wallace. Although his crew was still in Georgia finishing up the restoration of an antebellum mansion, he and his wife and their kids had returned to Charisma for the family event.

"It's a good thing your parents have a huge backyard," Cassie said, when they arrived at Ellen and John's residence.

"And that the weatherman was wrong in forecasting rain for today," Braden noted.

She looked up at the clear blue sky. "I guess even Mother Nature knows not to mess with Ellen Garrett's plans."

He chuckled. "You might be right about that."

As they made their way around the gathering, he introduced her to his aunts, uncles and cousins. When they crossed paths with Ellen, who was in her glory with so many little ones underfoot, she immediately whisked Saige away to play with her cousins. It seemed that everywhere Cassie looked, there were children and babies. And more than one expectant mother in the crowd, too.

Not long after they'd arrived, John dragged Braden away to man one of the extra grills that had been set up in the backyard. He was reluctant to leave Cassie's side, but she assured him that she would be fine. Although the words were spoken with more conviction than she felt, he took them at face value and accepted the chef's apron and long-handled spatula his father gave him.

"There's a gate by the garage," a pretty dark-haired woman said to her.

"Sorry?"

"You had that slightly panicked look in your eyes, as if you were searching for the nearest exit."

"Oh." Cassie blew out a breath and managed a smile. "I guess I am feeling a little overwhelmed. And I'm sorry—I know Braden introduced us, but I don't remember your name."

"Tristyn," the other woman said. "And there's no need to apologize. I sometimes feel overwhelmed at these gatherings, too, and I'm related to all of these people."

"When Braden said the whole family would be here, I didn't realize what that meant."

"There are a lot of us," his cousin agreed. "More and more every year, with all the babies being born."

"Do any of the little ones belong to you?"

"No," Tristyn said quickly, firmly. "I'm just a doting aunt—actual and honorary—to all of the rug rats running around."

The words were barely out of her mouth when a preschooler raced over to them, giggling as he was chased by a chocolate Lab that was as big as the child. Tristyn swept the little boy up into her arms and planted noisy kisses on each of his cheeks.

The dog plopped on its butt at their feet, tail swiping through the grass and tongue hanging out of its mouth.

Since Tristyn was fussing over the child, Cassie dropped to her knees beside the dog. Pleased with the attention, she immediately rolled onto her back. "Aren't you just the cutest thing?" she said, dutifully rubbing the animal's exposed belly.

The dog showed her agreement by swiping Cassie's chin with her tongue.

She chuckled softly. "Who does she belong to? And will they notice if I take her home with me?"

"What do you think, Oliver?" Tristyn asked the boy. "Would you notice if Cassie took Coco home with her?"

Oliver nodded solemnly.

"Well, as adorable as she is, I would never want to come between a boy and his dog," Cassie said.

"But there is supposed to be a leash between the boy and his dog," a different female voice piped up.

Cassie turned to see Braden's sister-in-law Harper with the leash in hand.

"But Coco wanted to meet Cassie," Oliver told her.

"Is that so?" his mother said, a smile tugging at her lips as she glanced at Cassie. "And have they been properly introduced now?"

Oliver nodded. "Coco gave her kisses and she didn't say 'yuck.'"

"That doesn't mean her kisses aren't yucky," Harper noted, bending down—not an easy task with her pregnant belly impeding her—to clip the leash onto the dog's collar. "Just that Cassie has better manners than your dog."

Coco looked at Harper with big soulful eyes, silently reproaching her for putting restrictions on her freedom.

She handed the leash to her son. "Please take her into the house so that she's not underfoot while Grandpa's grilling. And don't bug Grandma for a snack before dinner."

The little boy sighed but obediently trotted away with the dog in tow.

Harper watched him go, then her gaze shifted to encompass all of the people gathered in the backyard. "Now that we're back in Charisma, I find myself wondering how we ever stayed away so long."

"It might have had something to do with your contract with WMBT and *Mid-Day Miami*," Tristyn noted.

Harper nodded. "And maybe it was the right move for us at the time, but now…I'm so glad we're home."

"We all are," Tristyn told her. "If you'd stayed in Florida to have that baby, there would have been a convoy of Garretts down the I-95."

The expectant mother laughed. "Somehow, I don't doubt it," she said, then she turned her attention to Cassie. "Is this your first family event?"

Cassie nodded. "I've known Ellen for years and, through her, Saige since she was about six months old, but I only met Braden in March."

"The man moves fast," his sister-in-law noted, a suggestive sparkle in her eye.

Cassie felt her cheeks heat and hoped the reaction might be attributed to the afternoon sun. "We're friends," she said.

"Uh-huh," Harper agreed, smiling.

"It's true," Tristyn piped up in Cassie's defense. Or so she thought until the other woman spoke again. "In fact, they were very friendly in the shed just a little while ago."

"We were looking for a soccer ball for the kids," Cassie explained.

"And Braden thought a soccer ball might be hiding in your clothes?"

Now her cheeks weren't just hot, they were burning.

Harper chuckled but showed mercy by shifting her cousin's attention away from Cassie. "I'm going to make sure Coco isn't tripping up everyone in the kitchen."

"I should probably go in, too," Cassie said. "To give Ellen a hand."

"She has all the help she needs in the kitchen," Tristyn assured her. "The aunts have been managing family get-togethers for more years than I've been alive, and the meal preparation is more expertly choreographed than the dancers in a Beyoncé video."

Cassie couldn't help but smile at the mental image the other woman's words evoked. "I don't doubt that's true."

"The bar, on the other hand, looks abandoned," Tristyn said, linking her arm through Cassie's and guiding her in that direction.

"We're going to work the bar?"

Braden's cousin grinned. "No, we're going to get you a drink to accompany the dish I'm going to give you on my cousin."

Chapter Fifteen

Cassie would gladly have paid admission to spend a Day with the Garrett Clan—as Braden referred to it. It was a little chaotic and a lot of fun and she loved watching the interactions of his family. There was also much talking and teasing and more food than she'd ever seen in one place in her life. So she ate and she mingled and she found herself falling even more in love—not just with the man but with his whole family.

It was hard to keep track of who were siblings and who were cousins, because they were all "aunt" and "uncle" to little ones. Cassie had no experience with close-knit families like the Garretts. Growing up, she vaguely remembered a set of grandparents in Utah—her father's parents—who had sent cards at Christmas and on birthdays, but they'd both died a couple of years before Amanda did. Her mother had refused to talk about her family, so if she had any relatives on that side, Cassie had never known them.

For almost two years, the first two years after her mom had married Ray, Cassie had felt as if she was part of a real family. For the first time that she could remember, she'd lived with both a mother and a father, her sister and two stepbrothers, and it had been nice. Normal.

Even when she'd cringed at demonstrations of Ray's temper, she'd thought that was normal because she'd never really known anything different. But this was even better than that—this was the family she'd always dreamed of having someday, and being here with Braden gave her hope that the dream might be within her grasp.

"You sure do know how to throw a party," Cassie said to the hostess, when Ellen brought out a fresh pitcher of sweet tea and set it on the table with a stack of plastic glasses.

Braden's mom beamed proudly. "It's always fun getting the family together."

"It's nice that they could all be here," she commented. And she meant it. She envied Braden having grown up with Ellen and John as parents, and she was glad that Saige, despite not having a mother, would grow up secure in the knowledge that she was loved.

"Family means a lot to all of us," Ellen said. "And although I understood why Ryan and Harper wanted to move to Florida, I can't deny that—for the past three years—I've felt as if a part of my heart was missing."

"I guess a mother never stops worrying about her children—even when they have children of their own."

"That's the truth," Ellen confirmed. "But now that all of my boys are home and happy, I'm looking forward to focusing on and enjoying my grandchildren—and maybe planning another wedding in the not-too-distant future."

Cassie suspected that Ellen was hoping for some insights about her relationship with Braden, but she had none to give her. "Speaking of your grandchildren," she said, because she didn't dare comment on the latter part of Ellen's remark, "it looks like Saige wore more ice cream than she ate. I'm going to wash her up before she puts her sticky fingers on everything."

"There's a change table in the first bedroom at the top of the stairs," Ellen told her.

"Great," Cassie said, then scooped up the little girl and made her escape.

Braden was catching up with his middle brother when he caught a glimpse of Saige out of the corner of his eye. She'd been sitting on a blanket spread out on the grass with several other kids, all of them enjoying ice-cream sandwiches under the watchful eye of Maura, one of the oldest cousins. Having finished her frozen treat, Saige stood up and turned toward the house. He saw then that she hadn't actually eaten her dessert but painted her face and shirt with it.

He started to excuse himself to take her inside to wash up, but before he could interrupt Justin's ER story, he saw Cassie pick up his daughter and carry her toward the house. He couldn't hear what she said, but whatever it was, it made Saige giggle.

He never got tired of watching Cassie with Saige. She was so good with his daughter, so easy and natural. The first day he'd attended Baby Talk at the library, he'd been impressed by her humor and patience. If there was ever a woman who was meant to be a mother—and hopefully Saige's mother—it was Cassie.

"You haven't heard a word I've said," Justin accused.

"What?"

His brother shook his head. "Never mind."

"Why are you grinning?" Braden asked suspiciously.

"Because I never thought I'd see you like this," Justin admitted.

"Like what?" Braden asked.

"Head over heels. And—more important—happy."

He scowled. "What are you talking about?"

"I don't know if you really thought you were fooling anyone, but we could all tell that you were miserable in the last few years of your marriage, at least until Saige came along."

Braden couldn't deny it.

"It's nice to see you happy again," Justin said. "And if Cassie's the reason for that, you'd be smart to hold on to her."

"I intend to," he said, and headed into the house.

He found Cassie in the nursery—formerly Ryan's childhood bedroom that his parents had redone in anticipation of their first grandchild. It had been several more years before they'd actually needed it, but the room was in frequent use now whenever Ellen and John looked after Vanessa for Justin and Avery, or—even more frequently—Saige for Braden. In fact, his parents were talking about adding a second crib and a couple of toddler beds to ensure they'd be able to accommodate all of the grandchildren now that Ryan and Harper were back in Charisma with Oliver and another baby on the way.

"I wondered where you disappeared to," Braden said to Cassie.

She glanced over and smiled at him. "Saige had ice cream all over her, so I brought her in to wash up and change her clothes, then she started yawning and I realized it was getting close to her bedtime, so I decided to put her pajamas on her instead."

"You could have asked me to do it," he protested.

"You were busy with your brother, and I didn't mind," she said, as she fastened the snaps of Saige's one-piece sleeper.

The little girl lifted her arms, indicating her desire to be picked up. As soon as Cassie had done so, Saige laid her head on her shoulder and closed her eyes.

"I think all the excitement today has worn her out," Cassie said.

"No doubt," he agreed. "How about you?"

"I had a great day," she said. "I really enjoyed being here, watching you with your family. It's rare to see so many members of three different generations and all of them so close."

He lifted Saige from her arms and carried his daughter over to the crib, setting her gently down on the mattress, before turning back to Cassie again. "I'm glad that Saige has cousins of a similar age, although I haven't given up hope that she might have a brother or a sister—or both—someday, too."

"You should have more kids," Cassie said. "You're a wonderful father."

"Thanks, but first I'd have to find a woman who's willing to take on the challenges of a widower and his adopted daughter."

"I don't think you'll have too much trouble with that," she said, her tone light and teasing. "Your little girl is pretty darn cute."

"What about her dad?" he prompted.

Cassie smiled. "He's not hard to look at, either."

"Of course, she'd also have to be willing to put up with my family."

"Your family is wonderful," she assured him.

"Most of the time," he agreed. "I'm glad to see that you survived your first Garrett family gathering without any visible signs of trauma."

"First?"

He took her hands and linked their fingers together. "I

hope it's only the first of many, because being here with you today, I realized that this is where you belong—with me and Saige."

And then he released one of her hands to reach into the side pocket of his cargo shorts and pull out a small velvet box.

Cassie's eyes went wide when he offered it to her, but she made no move to take it.

So he flipped open the hinged lid with his thumb, revealing a princess-cut diamond solitaire set on a simple platinum band. "I'm asking you to marry me, Cassie. To be my wife and a mother to my daughter—and any other children we may have."

She stared at the ring in his hand, stunned.

Because while she had undeniably thought about the possibility of a future with Braden and Saige, she'd counseled her eager heart to be patient. Even if she believed Braden's claim that he wasn't still mourning the death of his wife, he'd experienced a lot of changes in his life over the past seventeen months and she didn't imagine that he was eager to make any more right now. And although he'd recently hinted that he was falling for her, she hadn't expected this.

"I know it's fast," he acknowledged, when she failed to respond. "And if it's too soon, I can wait. But I don't want to wait. I want to start the rest of my life with you as soon as possible."

And with those words, her heart filled with so much joy, her chest actually ached. "I want that, too," she finally said.

His lips curved then, and the warmth and happiness in his smile arrowed straight to her heart. Maybe this was fast—certainly a lot faster than she'd expected—but it felt so right. And when he took her hand and slid the ring onto her finger, it fit right, too.

* * *

"I didn't think we were ever going to get away," Braden said, when they finally left his parents' house a few hours later.

"It's your own fault," Cassie told him. "After you announced our engagement, your mother insisted on opening half a dozen bottles of champagne, and then everyone wanted to toast to something."

"Maybe I should have waited for a more private venue," he acknowledged. "But seeing you with my family today, how perfectly you fit, I knew there wouldn't be a more perfect moment.

"And Tristyn, in particular, was thrilled about the engagement, because our impending wedding plans ensure that the focus of attention will be shifted away from her, at least until after the ceremony."

"Is she usually the focus of attention?"

"Only since Lauryn and Ryder got married," he told her.

"And her other sister, Jordyn, is the artist married to Marco Palermo and who has the twin boys?"

"You must have been taking notes," he mused.

"A notebook would have come in handy," she told him. "Because not fifteen minutes after meeting Tristyn, I couldn't remember her name."

"Well, I'm impressed," he said. "And the combination of Lauryn's recent wedding with Jordyn's pregnancy has everyone wanting to know when Tristyn's going to settle down."

"But she's with Josh, right?"

Braden scowled. "Where did you ever get that idea?"

"From the fact that he didn't take his eyes off her the whole day."

The furrow in his brow deepened. "Really?"

"Or maybe I just assumed they were together, because

everyone else was paired up," she offered as an alternate explanation, attempting to appease him.

"Well, they're not together," he assured her. "Josh is a friend of Daniel's and his partner in Garrett/Slater Racing."

"So is Tristyn the only one who isn't married?"

"No, Nora is single, too, but her half-sister status provides a little bit of insulation from most of the familial nosiness," he told her.

"They're not nosy," she protested. "They're interested."

"Wait until they all want to help plan the wedding—then you can let me know if they're interested or interfering."

Cassie didn't get a chance to announce her engagement to her coworkers on Monday, because as soon as Stacey saw the ring on her finger, she squealed with excitement—an instinctive reaction that prompted a fierce shushing from Helen. She immediately grabbed Cassie's arm and dragged her into the staff room where they could talk without fear of reprisal.

"Ohmygod," Stacey said, her gaze riveted on the rock. "Is that thing real?"

"I haven't actually tried to cut glass with it, but I assume so," Cassie told her friend.

"Braden?"

"No, Mr. Pasternak," she said dryly, giving the name of one of their oldest patrons, who had a habit of falling asleep in the magazine section.

Stacey rolled her eyes. "Okay—stupid question. But when? Where? How?"

She smiled at the barrage of questions, happy to share the details and some of her own euphoria. "Last night. During a barbecue at his parents' house."

"He proposed to you in front of everyone?"

She shook her head. "No, it was just me and Braden. And Saige—but she was sleeping."

Her friend sighed dreamily. "So...when's the wedding?"

"We haven't set a date yet."

"What are you thinking—summer? Fall?"

"I really haven't had a chance to think about it," Cassie admitted. "Everything has happened so fast. In fact, when I woke up this morning, I had to look at my finger to be sure it wasn't a dream."

"It's a dream come true," Stacey said. "You're going to be Braden Garrett's wife and a mother to his baby girl." She sighed again. "Who would have guessed, the first day he came in here, that you'd be engaged to him less than three months later?"

"Everything did happen fast, didn't it?"

"Love doesn't have any particular timetable," Stacey said. "It's more about the person than the days."

Cassie rolled her eyes. "Are you giving me Pinterest advice now, too?"

"No, that's something I learned from my own experience," her friend said. "I knew that when you met the right man, he would love you as much as you love him."

Cassie smiled at that, but as she glanced at her engagement ring, the usual joy was tempered by doubts and questions.

And when she sat back down at her desk to prepare the schedule for the kids' summer reading club, Stacey's words echoed in the back of Cassie's mind, making her wonder: Did Braden love her as much as she loved him?

Did he love her at all?

Because now that she was thinking about it, she couldn't recall that he'd ever actually spoken those words to her. Not even after they'd made love, when she'd been snuggled in his embrace and whispered the words to him. Instead, he'd kissed her again, and she'd assumed that was proof he felt the same way. Now she wasn't so sure—and she hated the uncertainty.

But she pushed aside her worries and concerns. After all, a lot of men weren't comfortable putting their feelings into words. The fact that he'd asked her to marry him told her everything that she needed to know about his feelings.

Still, she was immensely grateful when a trio of seventh graders came in and asked her to help them find some books for a research project and she was able to focus on something other than the words Braden had never spoken.

It was nearly three weeks after the barbecue at his parents' house before Braden saw Ryan again. Of course, he knew his youngest brother was busy getting his family settled into a new house and transferring his job back to his old office, so he was pleased when Ryan showed up at his door after dinner on Wednesday night.

"There's a Prius in your driveway," Ryan noted.

Braden smiled. "Yeah, it's Cassie's car."

"Has she moved in with you then?"

"No," he admitted. "So far I've only managed to persuade her to bring a few things over, but she's sleeping here most nights."

"Does that mean I've come at a bad time?" his brother wondered.

"It depends on what you want."

"A beer?"

"I've got a few of those," he agreed. "Come on in."

Ryan followed him to the kitchen, where Braden took two bottles from the fridge and twisted off the caps, then handed one to his brother.

"Are you settled into the new house?"

"Mostly," Ryan said, following him out onto the back deck. "Of course, it's a lot bigger than the condo we had in Florida, so some of the rooms are still empty."

"Too bad there isn't a furniture store anywhere in this town," Braden said dryly.

Ryan grinned as he settled back in an Adirondack chair, his legs stretched out in front of him. "Yeah, Harper's already been to the showroom three times."

"She doesn't like anything?"

"She likes *everything.*"

"Well, maybe we'll set you up with a friends and family discount."

"Speaking of friends and family—"

"Why do I sense that you're now getting to the true purpose of your visit?"

Ryan tipped his bottle to his lips, drank. "Maybe it's none of my business—Harper told me it's none of my business," he admitted.

"It's generally good advice to listen to your wife," Braden told him.

"It probably is, but I can't deny that I'm a little worried you're rushing into marriage with Cassie."

He frowned at that. "Do you have a problem with my fiancée?"

"No," his brother quickly assured him. "She's great. In fact, she just might be perfect for you."

"Then why the concern?" he asked warily.

"Because I know you haven't known her very long. And because I know you were unhappy in the last few years of your marriage to Dana. And because you told me, after her funeral, that you felt guilty about failing in your promise to Saige's birth mom to give her daughter a real family."

"I'm still not seeing your point," he said, although he was beginning to suspect that he did.

"I can't help wondering—are you marrying Cassie because you want her for your wife? Or because you want her to be Saige's mother?"

"Considering that our marriage will put her in both of those roles, why do the reasons matter?" Braden countered. "And why are you in my face about this when you got married to give Oliver a family?"

"Because Oliver's aunt was suing for custody and we needed to ensure that he stayed with us, because that's what his parents wanted."

"And Saige's birth mother wanted her to have two parents—to grow up in a real family. And just as you would do anything for your son, I will do anything for my daughter."

"The difference being that when Harper and I decided to get married, we both knew why we were doing it."

"I want to marry Cassie," Braden assured his brother. "She's an incredible woman—warm and kind and generous. And Saige absolutely adores her."

"But do you love her?" Ryan pressed.

He tipped his bottle to his lips. "I will honor the vows I make to her on our wedding day," he finally said.

His brother shook his head, clearly unsatisfied with that answer. "She's in love with you, Braden. How long do you think it's going to take her to figure out that her feelings aren't reciprocated? And," he continued without giving Braden an opportunity to respond, "what do you think she'll do when she figures it out?"

"Getting married will give us both what we want," Braden insisted.

"I hope you're right," Ryan said. "Because losing another mother will be a lot harder on your daughter than growing up without one."

* * *

Cassie stood by the open window in Saige's bedroom, frozen by the conversation that drifted up from the deck as she lifted Braden's sleepy daughter into her arms. She'd just finished reading a story to the little girl and intended to take her downstairs to say good-night to her daddy when she heard voices from below and realized that he had company.

She hadn't intended to eavesdrop, but she couldn't avoid overhearing their conversation—and couldn't stop listening when she realized that they were talking about her.

I want to marry Cassie. She's an incredible woman—warm and kind and generous. And Saige absolutely adores her.

But do you love her?

Her breath caught as she waited for Braden to reply.

I will honor the vows I make to her on our wedding day.

The response answered not just his brother's question but her own, and with those few words, the joy leaked from her wounded heart like air from a punctured tire.

How long do you think it's going to take her to figure out that her feelings aren't reciprocated?

Well, Ryan's conversation with his brother had taken care of that for her. While she'd managed to disregard her own niggling doubts for the past few weeks, she could do so no longer.

And what do you think she'll do when she figures it out?

Cassie forced herself to move away from the window, but she couldn't force herself to answer that question. She didn't want to answer that question. She didn't want to do anything except go back ten minutes in time and never overhear Braden and Ryan's conversation.

Because she could live with her own doubts and uncertainties. As long as she had Braden and Saige, she could live with almost anything. But the one thing she could not live with was the absolute knowledge that the man she planned to marry—the man she loved with her whole heart—didn't love her back.

Unshed tears burned the back of her eyes as she rocked Saige to sleep for what she knew might be the very last time. She couldn't blame Braden. There had been so many clues as to his motivation—most notably Lindsay's visit and her threat to have the adoption revoked—but Cassie had refused to see them.

I will do anything for my daughter.

She'd always known he wanted a mother for Saige— he'd made no secret of that fact. But she'd let herself hope and believe that he wanted her, too. That when he took her in his arms and made love to her, it was because he did love her.

I will honor the vows I make to her...

An admirable sentiment but not the words she'd wanted to hear. Not what she needed from him.

Saige exhaled a shuddery sigh as her thumb slipped out of her mouth, a signal that the little girl was truly and deeply asleep. Cassie reluctantly pushed herself out of the chair and touched her lips to the top of the baby's head before she gently laid her in the crib and tucked her sock monkey under her arm.

Then she walked across the hall to Braden's room and the bed that she'd shared with him almost every night for the past several weeks. Peering through the window, she saw that his brother's car was still in the driveway. Though it was much earlier than she usually went to bed, she put on her pajamas, picked up a book and crawled between the covers. And when Braden finally came upstairs, she pretended to be asleep.

She heard his footsteps cross the floor, then he gently removed the book from her hand and set it on "her" bedside table before turning off the lamp. He moved away again, and she heard the quiet click of the bathroom door closing. A few minutes later, he crawled into bed with her, his arm automatically snaking around her waist and drawing her close, nestling their bodies together like spoons.

She'd been surprised to discover that he liked to sleep snuggled up to her. He protested, vehemently, when she accused him of being a cuddler, so she stopped teasing him because it didn't matter what he called it—the simple truth was that she slept so much better when she was in his arms. It was something that had become a habit far too easily and one that she would have to break. But not tonight.

It didn't take long for his breathing to settle into the slow, regular rhythm that told her he'd succumbed to slumber. And only then, when she was certain he was sleeping, did she let her tears fall, confident that they would dry by morning, leaving no evidence of her heartbreak on the pillowcase.

Chapter Sixteen

It was harder than she'd thought it would be to go through the motions the next day. She was distracted and unfocused at work, unable to concentrate on the most menial tasks. Though she hated to do it, she called Stacey to cover the Soc & Study group that night so that she could take some time at home and figure out her life and her future.

Truthfully, she knew what she had to do, but that didn't make the doing any easier. She loved Braden and Saige and she wanted nothing more than to be part of their family. She wanted to marry the man she loved, but she couldn't marry a man who didn't love her.

She needed to talk to Braden about the conversation she'd overheard, and she didn't want to fall apart when she did. So she spent the afternoon at home with her cats, trying to prepare herself for the inevitable confrontation. But whenever she thought about saying goodbye, the tears would spill over again. When she reached for a tissue to wipe her nose, Buttercup jumped up onto the sofa and crawled into Cassie's lap—which only made her cry harder. And Westley, who rarely paid attention to anything that wasn't dinner, eventually took pity on her and crawled into her lap beside his sister, too.

She gave them tinned food for dinner, because she figured they deserved a reward for their unsolicited support and comfort. And as she watched them chow down, she decided that maybe being a crazy cat lady wasn't so bad.

When they were finished eating, she knew that she'd stalled as long as she could. She dried her eyes again, got into her car and drove to Forrest Hill.

"I thought you had the Soc & Study group tonight," Braden said when he responded to the doorbell and found her standing on the porch. "And why didn't you use your key?"

"Stacey agreed to fill in for me," she said, ignoring the second part of his comment.

He stepped away from the door. "Are you hungry? Saige and I ate a while ago, but I can heat up some leftover lasagna for you."

She shook her head. "No, thanks."

"Well, I'm glad you're here," he said, his tone as sincere as the smile that tugged at her heart. "I got official notice from the court today that Lindsay withdrew her application to reverse the adoption."

"Oh, Braden, that is wonderful news," she said, genuinely thrilled that he wouldn't have to battle for custody of his daughter.

"And to celebrate, Saige has been working on something for you."

At that revelation, her carefully rehearsed words stuck in her throat. "For me?"

"Uh-huh." He took her hand and led her into the living

room where the little girl was playing at the train table. "Look who's here, Saige."

The toddler looked up, her lips immediately stretching into a wide smile when she saw Cassie. "Ma-ma."

Cassie instinctively squeezed Braden's hand as her throat constricted and her eyes filled with tears. Then she remembered why she was here, and she extricated her fingers from his.

"P'ay?" Saige asked hopefully.

"Not right now, sweetie."

Braden lifted a hand and gently brushed away the single tear that she hadn't realized had escaped to slide down her cheek. "What's wrong, Cassie?"

She could only shake her head, because her throat was too tight for words.

He took her hand again and led her to the sofa. "Tell me what's going on. Please."

She drew in a slow, deep breath and lifted her gaze to his. "I need to ask you something."

"Anything," he said.

"Do you love me?"

He drew back, instinctively and physically, which she recognized as his answer even before he said anything.

"Where is this coming from?" he asked.

"It's a simple question," she told him.

"It's a ridiculous question," he said, obviously still attempting to dance around it. "I asked you to marry me— doesn't that tell you how I feel about you?"

"Maybe it should," she acknowledged. "But I'd still like to hear it."

"I want to spend my life with you," he told her, and he sounded sincere. But even if it was true, it wasn't a declaration of love.

"Because Saige needs a mother? Because I complete your family?"

"Where is this coming from?" Braden asked again, his uneasiness growing as she tossed out questions he wasn't sure he knew how to answer.

"I heard you talking to your brother last night," she admitted. "When you told him that you were marrying me to give Saige the family you'd promised she would have when you adopted her."

And to think that he'd actually been happy when his brother had moved back to town.

"Why is it wrong to want a family for my daughter?" he said, still hoping to sidestep her concerns and smooth everything over.

"It's not," she said. "In fact, many people would say it's admirable. Especially the lengths to which you're willing to go to give it to her."

"You're losing me," he told her. But even more frustrating was the realization that *he* was in danger of losing *her*.

"Maybe I'm almost thirty years old, maybe I won't ever have a better offer, but I want not just to fall in love, but to be loved in return. I want the fairy tale." She slid her engagement ring off and set it on the table. "And I'm not willing to settle for anything less."

The sadness and resignation in her tone slayed him as much as her removal of the ring he'd put on her finger. "Cassie—"

She shook her head. "Don't."

"Don't what?" he asked, torn between bafflement and panic.

"Don't tell me again that you care or that we're really good together. Don't tell me again that Saige adores me. Don't paint rosy pictures of the future we can have together." She looked at him, the tears in her eyes slicing like knives through his heart. "Please don't tempt me to settle for less than I deserve, because I love you so much I might be willing to do it."

She was right. As much as Braden didn't want to admit it, she was right. When he'd asked her to marry him, he'd been selfish. He'd been thinking only of what he wanted—for himself and his daughter. He'd wanted to give Saige the security of the family that he knew they could be if Cassie agreed to be his wife.

And all the while that he'd been courting her, he'd known that he wasn't going to fall in love with her. It was no defense that he'd warned her against falling in love with him—because he'd then done everything in his power to make her forget that warning.

She did deserve more—so much more than he could give her. Because it was the only thing left to say, he finally said, "I'm sorry."

"So am I," she told him. Then, with tears still shining in her eyes, she turned and walked away.

And he let her go.

"Ma-ma?" Saige said as the door closed behind Cassie.

With a sigh, Braden lifted her into his lap and hugged her tight.

Losing another mother will be a lot harder on your daughter than growing up without one.

"I guess your uncle Ryan is smarter than he looks," he said regretfully.

But he knew the emptiness he felt inside wasn't just for Saige. An hour earlier, he'd been looking toward his future with Cassie and his heart had been filled with hope and joy. Now he was looking at the ring she'd taken off her finger and he felt as cold and empty as the platinum circle on the glass table.

* * *

Megan dropped a pile of bridal magazines on Cassie's desk when she came into the library Friday morning. "I've been planning my wedding for years and since I'm not any closer to finding a groom now than when I started, I thought you might want to look through these to get some ideas for your big day."

"Thanks," Cassie said. "But I'm not going to need them."

"Don't you dare tell me you're planning to elope," Megan warned.

"No, we're not planning to elope."

"You're hiring a wedding planner," was her coworker's second guess.

Cassie shook her head. "We're not getting married."

Her friend stared at her, stunned. "What are you talking about?"

"I gave Braden back his ring last night."

"What?" Megan's gaze dropped to her now-bare left hand. *"Why?"*

"Because I want to be someone's first choice."

Her friend frowned. "Is this because he was married before?"

"No. It's because he doesn't love me," she admitted softly, her heart breaking all over again to admit the truth aloud.

"Why would you say that?" Megan demanded.

"Because it's true."

"The man asked you to marry him," her coworker reminded her.

She nodded. "And fool that I was, it took me almost three weeks to realize that every time he talked about our future, he never once said that he loved me. Even when I said it first, he never said it back."

"A lot of men aren't comfortable with the words," Megan noted.

"A man who claims he's ready to commit himself in marriage should be."

Unable to dispute the truth of that, her friend picked up the pile of magazines again. "I'll put these in the staff room...just in case."

Cassie didn't argue, but she knew there wasn't going to be any "just in case." She also knew that the awkward and difficult conversation with Megan was only the first of many she would have over the next few weeks.

The problem with sharing the happy news of her engagement with so many people was that she had to either pretend she was still happily engaged—albeit not wearing a ring—or admit that the shortest engagement in the history of the world was over.

Okay, she knew that was probably an exaggeration. After all there were plenty of celebrity marriages that hadn't even lasted as long as her engagement. Or at least one, she mentally amended, thinking of Britney Spears's famous fifty-five hour nuptials.

Of course, everyone had words of advice ranging from "give him another chance" to "you'll find someone else." Cassie knew they meant well, but no advice could heal a heart that was cracked wide-open.

Almost as bad as the aching emptiness in her chest was the realization that she dreaded going into work Tuesday morning. When she woke up, she wanted to pull the covers over her head and pretend that she was sick so she could stay home with her cats and avoid seeing Braden's mother and daughter. The apprehension was an uncomfortable weight in her belly, but it also helped her stiffen her spine. Because she loved her job and she wasn't going to let a failed relationship take that joy from her.

Still, she had to force a smile for her Baby Talk class. It was all she could do to hold back the tears when Saige released her grandmother's hand and ran to Cassie, wrapping herself around her legs, but she went through the motions. And because all of the caregivers were focused on their children, no one seemed to realize anything was wrong.

But after class had ended and everyone else was gone, Ellen approached her. Cassie braced herself, not sure what to expect from the woman she'd always liked and respected but who didn't understand the concept of boundaries. So she was surprised when Ellen didn't say anything about the failed engagement. In fact, she didn't say anything at all; she just reached for Cassie's hand as she walked past her on the way out, giving it a gentle but somehow reassuring squeeze.

If she was surprised by Braden's mother's discretion and unexpected show of support, she was even more surprised when Irene defended Braden, insisting that his feelings for Cassie were probably deeper than he was willing to acknowledge.

Cassie appreciated the sentiment but she refused to believe it, refused to let herself hope and have her hopes trampled again.

Braden didn't want to talk about the break-up with Cassie, so he didn't. Whenever anyone asked about her, he said she was doing great. If someone wanted to chat about the wedding, he just said they hadn't figured out any details yet. And while he knew the truth would eventually come out, he was feeling too raw to deal with it right now.

Of course, his mother didn't care about that.

"I'm a little confused," she said, when he picked Saige up after work on Tuesday. "On the weekend, we were talking about potential wedding venues, and then, when I took Saige to the library for Baby Talk today, I discovered that Cassie wasn't wearing her engagement ring."

"Maybe it needs to be sized," he suggested.

"Even if that was true, it doesn't explain why your supposed fiancée looked as if her heart was broken."

"I don't know why her heart would be broken," he grumbled, finally giving up the pretense that everything was status quo. "She was the one who decided to give me back the ring."

"And I've known Cassie long enough to know that she wouldn't have done so without a good reason, so what was it?"

He busied himself sorting through a pile of miscellaneous stuff—junk mail, flyers and the book Cassie had lent to him from her personal library—on the kitchen island. "Because I didn't echo the words back when she told me that she loved me," he finally admitted.

Ellen frowned. "And why didn't you?"

"Because I was trying to be honest about my feelings and I didn't want our marriage to be based on a deception."

His mother stared at him for several long seconds before she let out a weary sigh. "Now I see the problem."

"I'm not going to fall in love again."

She shook her head. "The problem is that you actually believe that's true."

"Because it *is* true," he insisted.

"Honey, you wouldn't be this miserable if you didn't love her."

He set the book on top of the pile so that he could return it to her. Except she might think he was using the book as an excuse to see her again—and maybe he would be. "I'm miserable because I let my daughter down. Again."

"If that's your biggest concern, maybe you should give Heather Turcotte a call," Ellen suggested. "She was asking about you at the library again today."

"Geez, Mom, can you give me five minutes to catch

my breath before you start tossing more potential Mrs. Garretts at me?"

"Why do you need time?" his mother challenged. "If you aren't in love with Cassie—if all you want is a mother for Saige—why aren't you eager to move ahead toward that goal?"

He opened his mouth, closed it again. "I really am an idiot, aren't I?"

"As much as it pains me to admit it—in this situation— I have to answer that question with a resounding yes."

He sighed. "What am I supposed to do now?"

"You figured out how to screw it up all by yourself, I have faith that you can figure out how to fix it."

He sincerely hoped she was right.

Braden knew that after refusing to say the words Cassie had wanted to hear, she would doubt their veracity when he said them to her now. But how was a man supposed to prove his feelings? What kind of grand gesture would convince her how much she meant to him?

It took him a while to come up with a plan—and a lot longer to be able to implement it. So it was almost three weeks after she'd given him back his ring before he was ready to face her again—to put his heart and their future on the line.

The moment Cassie saw him waiting on her porch, her steps faltered. He forced himself to stay where he was, to wait for her to draw nearer, but it wasn't easy. The last few weeks without her had been the emptiest weeks of his life, and he wanted nothing more than to take her in his arms and just hold her for a minute. An hour. Forever.

She came up the stairs slowly, pausing beside the front door. "What are you doing here, Braden?"

"I needed to talk to you and you haven't returned any of my calls."

"Maybe I didn't return your calls because I didn't want to talk to you," she suggested.

"I considered that possibility," he acknowledged. "But it's not in my nature to give up that easily."

"Where's Saige?"

"With my parents. I didn't want this to be about anything but you and me."

"I have things to do," she said. "So please say whatever you need to say and then go."

"I love you, Cassie."

She looked away, but not before he saw the shimmer of tears in her eyes. She didn't say anything for a long moment, and then she shook her head. "It's not enough to say it—you have to mean it."

"But I *do* mean it," he told her. "I meant it even when I couldn't bring myself to say it, but I didn't want to admit the truth of my feelings because I'd promised myself that I wouldn't fall in love again.

"I want you in my life, Cassie. I *need* you in my life. I don't even care if you don't want to put the ring back on your finger—not yet. I want to marry you, I want to spend my life with you, and yes—I do want you to be Saige's mother because you're so great with her and I know how much she loves you. But most importantly, I just want to be with you, because my life is empty without you.

"When I finally realized I loved you, I tried to figure out why—what it was about you that made me fall in love with you. And I discovered that it wasn't any *one* thing— it was *every*thing. And every day I'm with you, I discover something new that makes me love you even more than the day before."

"You're doing it again," she whispered softly. "Saying all of the right things."

"But?" he reluctantly prompted, because he could hear the unspoken word in the tone of her voice.

"But you're a businessman. You know how to close a deal. I don't know if you really mean what you're saying or if you're saying it because you know it's what I want to hear."

"You have every reason to be wary," he acknowledged. "I'm asking you to trust in feelings that I wouldn't even acknowledge a few weeks ago."

She nodded.

"So give me a chance to prove my feelings are real," he suggested.

"How?" she asked, obviously still skeptical.

"Come home with me so that I can show you something."

Home.

The word wrapped around her like a favorite sweater— warm and comforting and oh-so-tempting.

Except that the home he was referring to wasn't her home, only where he lived with his daughter.

"The last time I fell for that line was my first year at college," she said, feigning a casualness she didn't feel.

"It's not a line," he assured her.

Cassie sighed, but her resistance had already crumbled. It wasn't just that she couldn't say no to him but that she didn't want to. She didn't want to shut him out—she wanted him to force open the doors of her heart and prove that he loved her.

She didn't know what, if anything, could make her trust that the feelings he claimed to have for her now were real, but she was willing to give him a chance. The past three weeks without him had been so achingly empty, because she loved him so much she wanted to believe a future for them was possible.

"I need to feed the cats," she said.

"I'll wait."

Cassie noticed the changes as soon as she stepped through the front door and into the wide foyer of Braden's house. The previously bland off-white walls had been painted a warm pale gold. The color was still subtle but it drew out the gold vein in the floor tile and provided a sharper contrast for the white trim.

The living room was a pale moss green and the furniture was all new—the off-white leather sofa and armchairs having been replaced by a dark green sectional with a chaise lounge, and the contemporary glass-and-metal occasional tables replaced by mission-style tables in dark walnut. The only piece of furniture that remained from her last visit was Saige's train table.

"End of season sale at Garrett Furniture?" she asked, her tone deliberately light.

"Something like that," he agreed.

"And the paint?"

"My cousin Jordyn. You seemed to like what she did in Saige's room, so I asked her to pick out the colors."

"She has a good eye," she noted.

As they continued the tour, she discovered that every single room—aside from Saige's—had been redone. Not all of them had new furnishings, but each had at least been repainted with decorative accents added.

"Why did you do all of this?"

"It's partly symbolic," he confessed. "To illustrate the warmth and color you brought back into my life. But it's mostly practical, because I hoped that if you actually liked my house you might want to spend more time here, and maybe reconsider moving in. Of course, if there's anything you don't like, we can change it. We can change everything, if you want."

"I do like your house," she told him. "And everything looks fabulous, but—"

"Hold that thought," he said. "There's still one more room to see."

She'd been so amazed by the changes he'd made throughout the house, she hadn't realized that he'd ushered her past the main floor den until he paused there now. He seemed more nervous about this room than any other, which made her even more curious about what was behind the closed doors.

"The painting was simple and, with a full crew of men working round the clock, pretty quick," he told her. "But I wanted some more significant changes made in this room—which is what took so long. Thankfully, Ryder put me in touch with the right people or I'd still be waiting."

Then he opened the doors.

The room, originally a simple main floor office with a desk and a few bookcases, had been transformed to include floor-to-ceiling bookcases, lots of comfortable seating and a fireplace that was almost an exact replica of the one in Cassie's living room.

She had to clear the lump out of her throat before she could speak. "The bookcases are empty," she finally said.

"Not completely," he said, taking her hand and drawing her over to a shelf between two windows where she could see a single book lying on its side: *The Princess Bride: S. Morgenstern's Classic Tale of True Love and High Adventure* by William Goldman.

"Did you read it?" she asked him.

He nodded. "I'm not sure I agree it was better than the movie, but it was a good book," he acknowledged.

"You did this for me—so that I would have a place in your house for my books?"

"*Our* house," he said. "You only have to say the word and it's our house."

"What word is that?"

He pulled his hand out of his pocket and showed her the ring she'd given back to him three weeks earlier. "Yes," he told her. "When I ask again, 'Will you marry me, Cassie?' you just have to say yes."

Then he dropped to one knee and took her hand in his. "Cassie MacKinnon, I love you with my whole heart, and there's nothing I want more in this world than to spend every day of the rest of my life with you by my side. Will you marry me?"

She held his gaze, her own steady and sure, and finally answered his question, not with a yes but with the words that came straight from her heart. "As you wish."

Epilogue

Every morning when she woke up in her husband's arms, Cassie took a moment to bask in the sheer joy of her new life.

In the five months that they'd been married, Braden had given her everything she'd ever wanted: a home, a family, love. He never missed a chance to tell her that he loved her, and though her heart still swelled each time she heard the words, he showed her the truth of those words in even more ways. Every day with Saige brought new joys and experiences, too. After waiting for so long to be a mother, Cassie was loving every minute of it.

On Valentine's Day, Cassie made a pork roast with sweet potatoes and parsnips, which Saige hated, followed by ice-cream sundaes, which Saige loved. After dinner, Braden presented Cassie with two gifts. A diamond-encrusted heart-shaped pendant and a homemade Valentine. The former was stunning, but the latter took her breath away: Braden's handprints—in red paint—were upside down and overlapped at the thumbs to form a big heart inside which Saige's handprints—in pink paint—formed a smaller heart. On the outside, making a border around the edge, he had written:

> *For Cassie—on our first Valentine's Day together with tons of love and thanks for being such a fabulous wife and mother and making our family complete. We love you more than you will ever know.*
> *Braden & Saige xoxoxoxoxo*

Cassie's eyes filled as she read the printed words, but she didn't know the tears had spilled over until Saige asked, "Why you cwyin', Mama?"

She wiped at the wet streaks on her cheeks. "Because I love both of you more than you will ever know, too," she said.

Of course, Saige continued to look perplexed. Braden dropped a kiss on the little girl's forehead and told her to go play with her trains. She skipped out of the room, happy to comply with the request.

"Cassie?" he prompted when their daughter had gone.

"Sometimes I can't believe how much my life has changed since I met you."

"But in a good way, right?"

She managed to smile. "In the very best way," she assured him.

He plucked a tissue from the box and gently dabbed at the streaks of moisture on her cheeks. "So these are... happy tears?"

She nodded.

"Okay," he said, obviously relieved.

"But I should warn you," Cassie said, lifting her eyes to his, "I think I'm going to be one of those women who is really emotional in the first trimester."

Braden stared at her for a minute, his hand dropping away from her face as the confusion in his gaze slowly gave way to comprehension and joy. "Are you saying…?"

They'd decided to stop using birth control as soon as they were married, because they didn't know how long it might take for Cassie to get pregnant and they were hoping that Saige would have a little brother or sister sooner rather than later—which was apparently going to happen even sooner than either of them had anticipated.

But she could understand why he'd be hesitant to ask the question. Although she didn't know all the details of everything he and Dana had gone through in their efforts to conceive a child, she knew how disappointed he'd been by their lack of success—and that he would, naturally, be reluctant to hope that it would happen now.

"Yes." She took his hand and laid it on her abdomen. "I'm pregnant."

He whooped and lifted her off the chair and into his arms, spinning her around in circles. Then he stopped abruptly and set her carefully back on her feet and framed her face with his hands. "Are you all right? Have you been to see a doctor? How are you feeling?"

She laughed, a little breathlessly, before she answered each of his questions in turn. "Yes. Not yet. Happy and excited and so incredibly lucky."

The grin that spread across his face assured her that he was feeling happy, too. Even if he still looked a little dazed.

"Wow. That was…fast," he decided.

"Too fast?" she wondered.

He immediately shook his head. "No, it's not too fast," he promised. "And this news is the second best Valentine's Day present ever."

She lifted her brows. "*Second* best?"

"Second best," he confirmed. Then he lowered his head to kiss her. Softly. Deeply. "Second only to you."

* * * * *

Look for Tristyn Garrett's story,
THE LAST SINGLE GARRETT,
*the next installment in award-winning author
Brenda Harlen's miniseries for
Harlequin Special Edition*
THOSE ENGAGING GARRETTS!
*On sale May 2017, wherever Harlequin books and
ebooks are sold.*

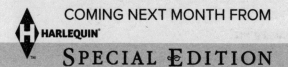
Available February 21, 2017

#2533 FORTUNE'S SECOND-CHANCE COWBOY
The Fortunes of Texas: The Secret Fortunes • by Marie Ferrarella
Young widow Chloe Fortune Eliot falls for Chance Howell, an ex-soldier with PTSD, but will their fear of another heartbreak stop them both from seizing a second chance at love?

#2534 JUST A LITTLE BIT MARRIED
The Bachelors of Blackwater Lake • by Teresa Southwick
Rose Tucker is a single woman with a failing business. Or so she thinks. Then her ex, Lincoln Hart, shows up with an offer for her design services...and the bombshell that a paperwork glitch makes them a little bit married.

#2535 KISS ME, SHERIFF!
The Men of Thunder Ridge • by Wendy Warren
Even as Willa Holmes vows not to risk loving again after a tragedy, she finds herself the subject of a hot pursuit by local sheriff Derek Neel. Can she escape the loving arm of the law? Does she even want to?

#2536 THE MARINE MAKES HIS MATCH
Camden Family Secrets • by Victoria Pade
Kinsey Madison has a strict policy about dating military men: she won't. Of course that means she can team up with Lieutenant Colonel Sutter Knightlinger to get his widowed mother settled and Kinsey in contact with her new family without risking her heart...right?

#2537 PREGNANT BY MR. WRONG
The McKinnels of Jewell Rock • by Rachael Johns
When anonymous advice columnist and playboy Quinn McKinnel receives a letter from Pregnant by Mr. Wrong, he recognizes the sender as Bailey Sawyer, his one-night-stand, and has to decide whether to simply fess up or win over the mother of his child.

#2538 A FAMILY UNDER THE STARS
Sugar Falls, Idaho • by Christy Jeffries
On a "glamping" trip for her magazine, Charlotte Folsom has a fling with her guide, Alex Russell. But back in Sugar Falls, they keep running into each other, and their respective families fill a void neither knew was missing. Will Charlotte and Alex be too stubborn to see the forest for the trees?

SPECIAL EXCERPT FROM

H HARLEQUIN®

™ SPECIAL EDITION

*A young widow falls for Chance Howell, an ex-soldier
with PTSD, but will Chloe Fortune Elliott's discovery
that she's linked to the famous Fortune family destroy
their chance at a future together?*

*Read on for a sneak preview of
the next book in* **THE FORTUNES OF TEXAS:
THE SECRET FORTUNES** *miniseries,
FORTUNE'S SECOND-CHANCE COWBOY,
by* USA TODAY *bestselling author Marie Ferrarella.*

Chance knew he should just go. Normally, he would have.
But something was making him dig in his heels and stay.
He wanted to get something straight.

"Is this the kind of stuff you're going to be feeding
those boys?" he asked. "Stuff about slaying dragons?"

"No, this is the kind of 'stuff' I'm going to be using
in order to try to understand the boys," she said. "To help
them reconnect with the world."

He laughed drily. Still sounded like a bunch of mumbo
jumbo to him.

"Well, good luck with that," he told her, shaking
his head. "But if you ask me, a little hard work and a
little responsibility should help those boys do all the
reconnecting that they need."

"Hard work and responsibility," she repeated, as if he
had just quoted scripture. "Has it helped you?" Chloe
asked innocently.

His scowl deepened for a moment, and then he just

waved her words away. "Don't try getting inside my head, Chloe Elliott. There's nothing in it for you. I'm doing just fine just the way I am."

She suppressed a sigh. "Okay, as long as you're happy."

Happy? When was the last time he'd been happy? He couldn't remember.

"Happy's got nothing to do with it," Chance answered. "I'm my own man on my own terms, and that's all that really counts."

He felt himself losing his temper, and he didn't want to do that. Once things were said, they couldn't get unsaid, and a lot of damage could be done. He didn't want that to happen. Not with this woman.

"I'd better go find the boss. Graham said that he wanted to take me around the spread as soon as I stashed my gear."

She didn't want to be the reason he was late. "Then I guess you'd better get going."

"Yeah, I guess I'd better." With that, he crossed back to the door.

He walked out feeling that there were things left unspoken. A great many things. But then, maybe it was better that way. He wasn't looking to have his head "shrunk" any more than it already was. Even if the lady doing the shrinking was nothing short of a knockout.

Some things, he reasoned, were just better off left alone.

Don't miss
FORTUNE'S SECOND-CHANCE COWBOY
by Marie Ferrarella,
available March 2017 wherever
Harlequin® Special Edition books and ebooks are sold.

www.Harlequin.com

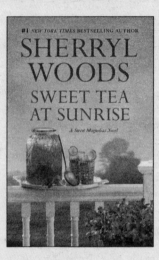